The
Backworlds

Book One

M. Pax

ISBN: 061568176X
ISBN-13: 978-0615681764

Cover by: edhgraphics
Graphic Artist Erin Dameron-Hill
www.edhgraphics.blogspot.com

Also by M. Pax

The Backworld Series
The Backworlds
Stopover at the Backworlds' Edge
Boomtown Craze

Hetty Locklear Series
The Renaissance of Hetty Locklear

Semper Audacia

The Tumbas
(Wandering Weeds Anthology)

Free Reads
Plantgirl
Small Graces
Translations

What readers are saying...

"I found Backworlds to be an interesting, well-written story that was a little different from some science fiction I have read. Overall it was entertaining and kept me reading until the end." *John T. Burch*

"I look forward to the next book in the series and reading other works by this author. " *Larry B. Gray*

"This book was a surprise and I would read more from this author. You will like it, too. It's just long enough to tell the story and not get bogged down in details." *Carl*

"The fast pace action goes from one edge of the galaxy to the other. This book is a page turner and you will not want to put it down." *E. Aaron Scott*

"There is plenty of action and a plethora of shady, underworld characters, and I never knew exactly which of Craze's friends and partners in crime to trust. Great. I like unpredictability. The Backworlds seems to be a den of thieves and conmen." *Graeme Ing*

"I was shushing everybody around me so I could read --a dashing tale of mischief and adventure. One word of warning--don't start reading this if you don't want to go ahead and read the next book. It's impossible; you're going to be hooked." *Maria T. Violante*

"I kept thinking as I read it that I hope this goes big--and is made into a TV series. The premise could outshine "Farscape" in entertainment value. Looking forward to the next in the series." *Teresa Cypher*

"Great job, M Pax. I thoroughly enjoyed the trip you took me on. I appreciated your characterization, the pacing, and how this new world was introduced without too much direct exposition and/or description. It was an easy-to-read page-turner, and I shall definitely be on the lookout for more of your works." *Julie*

"I really enjoyed this book. I have bought "the Stopover at the Backworlds' Edge" and will read that too and most likely any others that have these characters." *Greg1969*

"But it wasn't only the author's mastery of creating a believable universe that I enjoyed. The Story itself kept me glued to my Kindle even when chores were calling my name. Predictable storylines bore me. But M Pax keeps surprising me with twists and turns I didn't see coming. What a fun romp." *Retta Brown*

"The Backworlds is a great start on what should be a wonderful space opera series. It's a good, fast read that will leave you wanting more. I am certainly looking forward to the next installment." *Puna J*

ACKNOWLEDGMENTS

Continuing and many thanks to: Misha Gericke, Mike Rettig, Ella Zane, Dennis Strachota. Added thanks to Lindsay Buroker, Trudy Schoenborn, and Tony Benson.

And my life would be so much harder without the support of: Husband Unit, William Pax, Kimberly Nicole, my family and friends.

Thanks to all the fans who have rallied behind me. You're the best.

For Mom

I wrote you something.

✦ *Chapter 1*

Craze never imagined his pa would turn on him. Bast served up manipulation and cold calculation with cups of malt to strangers, to suckers, to fools, and competitors. Not to his son, not to anyone in the family.

Bast had always said, "Never trust a con." He pounded in the lessons until Craze could recite them inside-out and could smell a schemer from ten kilometers away. Craze should have known to ignore the one on how dodgy fathers don't count as cons, should've known Bast couldn't be trusted.

Craze snorted, glowering into the single malt. The wooden cup added to the flavor, deepening and enriching the magic carpet in the tumbler. Craze had dubbed it magic, because just a few swigs could transport him out of reality, even this horror pit his pa had just shoved him into.

"This world ain't big enough for both of us," his father had said while pouring the drink. "Time for you to find new opportunities. For us."

For us? Craze wanted to laugh. Shit. That kind of talk was for uncooperative members of the council of elders or business rivals.

Swirling the liquid smoke around his tongue, the fire mellowed into a flavor akin to pleasure. Craze let it trickle down his throat, savoring the burn trailing deep into his stomach. It staved off the damp and his father's chilling words, "Time for you to go, son."

They sat at the bar of the family tavern, sharing the end of the day as they often did. Only this time, they didn't conspire about how to rise in status among the Verkinn, or discuss which council elder they needed to manipulate into doing what. They didn't laugh over the saps they'd duped out of chips either. Years of acquiring chips and standing Craze had assumed would come into his hands, making that ancient saying about assumptions, older than Backworlder genes, right.

Craze found it hard to meet his father's gaze. His meaty fingers flicked over a corner of his tab— a data device the size and thinness of a card with funds transferred onto it. He stared at the figure. "That ain't much, Pa. Won't even buy me a place to piss."

Outside the window next to Craze's right elbow, dew settled as the sun sank among the tangled jungle of ganya tree leaves and branches, reaching high and low like an enormous bramble thicket. The moisture thickened, cloying as the day grew long, pooling into puddles, seeping in through the panes. The heaters couldn't keep out the cold of the coming night, couldn't warm up his pa's order for him to leave either.

The painful sentence echoed like bad hooch stuck in the digestive tract. Go where? Craze's chest constricted, his thoughts went round and round. He rubbed at the ache between his breasts and the one at his temples, hoping he'd heard his father wrong.

The malt numbed it some. He threw the rest of the drink back, licking off any remnants clinging to his fleshy lips. His dark eyes narrowed, studying his father. The man stood behind the bar like a boulder, his square jaw set, which widened the splay of his nose and cheeks that were so much like Craze's.

Everyone had always remarked on how much Craze and his pa were alike in appearance and manner. They could schmooze better than a slick-tongued peace negotiator bargaining a new truce, and they both had ebony hair and eyes, dusky skin, and an intimidating, beefy build. Craze used to take pride in that. In one moment, one sentence, it all changed. His father had broken the rules he'd set up between them. He'd sold his son in order to rise in the Verkinn elders' esteem. Craze swore right there and then to never become like his father, and he didn't want to do what his father asked of him, resented it'd been asked at all.

Tapping out the last droplets from the cup into his needy mouth, Craze held it out for a refill. His pa made the finest malt on all the Backworlds, drawing connoisseurs from all over the Lepper System—the portals of transportation the Backworlders traveled on. Craze would need a whole keg to deal with the words filling his flat, indistinct ears.

"I've saved money for this day," Bast said. "I know the startup fund ain't much, but it be enough for a position where you can make better 'n move on. You'll make the most of it. I know." He poured the equivalent of three shots into a cup, the malt gurgling pleasantly. "Then you 'n I will come to dominate the Backworlds. Folks wanting our malt, mead, and ale. Hollering for it everywhere. Telling us their secrets as they sip down our hooch, sometimes secrets we can profit from."

Bast toasted Craze, then swigged his finely-crafted booze. "Later, I'll send on your sisters with their families 'n more son's. You'll send out your offspring 'n the galaxy will be liquid resin in our hands. Moldable and shapeable to our whim. Yup, the boys of Bast will take the stars. Our..., your, your future is so bright, my boy."

His pa's chest swelled and his eyes gleamed as he gazed wistfully into the tomorrow he envisioned, lips twitching into a faint smile. "Talked the council elders into agreeing. So, this be sanctioned. Yup, you'll be the Verkinn's next great hero, spreading our people out in hopes you can make something amounting to success on what's left of the Backworlds. Make a statement our kind be not done. No, the Verkinn will rise again 'n you'll lead the way."

Craze heard nothing beyond the glory of Bast. "My leadin' greatly benefits you. So you hope."

His father frowned, spitting, starting to snarl. Then he fell quiet, saying nothing. Eyes brimming with moisture, he washed cups and wiped off bottles and kegs. His shoulders sagged. "If you

want to think me so low... after all we've shared...
I thought you knew me better, son."

Craze cradled his head in his large hands. Shit.
His father had kept him and taught him all these
years. Maybe his pa did mean well, did mean to
further Craze's standing in life. Craze wanted to
believe that more than his father turning on him.

"Where do you suggest I go, Pa? No other
suitable world's been found for us. Not for thrivin',
so the Verkinn council has said. As soon as I set
foot on another world, I'll go into hibernation if
the air isn't right."

"The council lied. They wanted the Verkinn all
in one place to regroup after the war. So our people
could grow strong again. I don't know where you
should go, but go you must. Many worlds won't be
suitable for you. The council 'n I planned for it
though." Bast leaned over, resting his elbows on
the counter. "We met a man with a mechanical
woman; she was a cybernetic Backworlder, an
engineer type. She invented a pair of coveralls
that'll keep the right amount of organics flowing in
your blood, enhancing whatever oxygen there be
on whatever world you end up on, keeping you
from hibernating if you don't wish to. The garment
be in your pack. See, I be looking out for you, my
boy."

His father thrust his chin at the corner by the
door where a canvas sack laid. Wrinkled and
deflated, the worn bag sank in on itself decreeing
not much was in it.

If they'd engineered a whole freaking garment to
keep Craze from hibernating in less ideal
environments, Bast and the council had known

about this day for some time. Just how long had they been planning this? Craze's stomach churned cold, creating a granule of ice in his center. He felt certain he'd never warm up.

A lantern sat on the bar between Craze and Bast. It flickered out of beat with the fire crackling in a pit in the center of the dim room. The tavern had been created from a ganya tree—intelligent flora that adored the Verkinn. The walls, floors, and ceiling spanned in a natural canopy, and the trunk twisted and arced as Craze's father had commanded, scented with a sweet spice inviting customers to hang around. The bar and shelves were formed from limbs crossing and braiding. They swathed the walls and counter in swirls. The bark had become smooth from years of being touched by Backworlders of all kinds, but most of all by the Verkinn. The tree had absorbed the softness of Verkinn flesh, making the trait its own.

His pa's living hair slicked itself back, taut and straight, pulling his wide face into an expression used to send unwelcome patrons out the door. Mixed messages. One second he was the loving father, the next a self-serving bastard. Which Bast did Craze deal with? A tiny inkling in the back of his mind whispered the slickster Bast was the true man standing there. No matter what Bast said or did, he served himself. Craze didn't really want to listen. There was comfort in thinking he dealt with the father. It wasn't to be though. Bast's sneer grew more menacing, belying all the good Craze wanted to put his faith into, showing the reality beyond the charismatic facade. The bastard.

The tavern belonged to Craze as much as to his

father. He wouldn't give up his position without a fight. He had his hair braid itself into a single plait, matching crusty expressions with Bast. "This is my place, Pa."

"No." His father folded his powerful arms over his barrel chest.

Craze had the same physique, so Bast's stature didn't intimidate him. Nor did the surly posture. Craze could take the older man on and win, therefore, he copied the stance and kicked the bar. The ganya tree trembled from the blow.

"All Verkinn live here. Here! Where am I to go?" he asked.

Bast grabbed at Craze's shirt, lifting him off the chair, growling. "Watch your manners. You ain't my only means of branching out. I can marry your sisters off to some saps who'll follow my every word. You do what I say, or I'll take the funds back 'n give you the boot anyway. You understand?"

Bastard plus two. Craze pulled out of his father's grasp, wheeling about to face the window. The setting sun twisted the glow of daylight, distorting colors in the village. Not so different from Bast lifting the veil over Craze's eyes. How had it come to this? Craze's fists balled.

Bast clapped Craze on the shoulder, an affectionate caress, a more fatherly gesture, which shifted the mood between them again. "Look, I know this be hard on you, but you need to toughen up. Become your own man. It's for the best. This be as far as you'll ever get on Siegna. You need to go off on your own. No more tagging on my sorry example. Follow the Lepper, talk to folks 'n you'll find something. You resourceful, son. You'll figure it out."

Craze softened under the loving touch and encouraging words. He glanced over his shoulder at a father. Maybe Bast really did mean well. Craze wanted it to be so.

His pa poured another shot of malt, handing it to Craze. Craze sipped the drink until it mellowed his gruff mood, replacing it with a growing trench of vulnerability induced by the flow of alcohol.

"It's good to know you believe in me, Pa. I'm not so sure though. Siegna's all I know. This tavern is all I know. How do I spread the Verkinn race among the Backworlds? There's no Verkinn out there by which to mate 'n start a village of my own. There'll just be me."

"I taught you well. You'll find your way. When you be settled 'n prospering, I'll send you a wife."

"Yerness?" Craze had been courting her the past year. The idea of leaving her brought on a wave of nausea. He wanted to run his hands over her curves again and feel the tickle of her laugh against his throat. He touched the spot on his neck her lips had last touched, cradling the memory of pleasure.

His father wouldn't meet his gaze, scrubbing at the sticky spots on the bar, washing and wiping, scouring past the filth into sawdust. Cold climbed all over Craze, inside and out.

"She's seein' somebody else, isn't she?" Craze had to know for sure what he'd be leaving behind. He punched the bar. The tree moaned. "Who?"

"It be for the best if you leave her alone. Just pick up your bag 'n go."

The words hit harshly, causing Craze to wince and pound on the bar top again. The tree growled.

He gulped down the malt and held the cup out for another.

His father waved a hand in refusal. "There be no time. Get the coveralls on 'n get going. Your transport to Elstwhere leaves in an hour."

"An hour? That's so sudden."

"A successful man puts his business—"

"First. I know, but—"

"You'll most like fall on your face some, but I taught you to keep getting up. Prosperity 'n success be found by getting up again 'n again 'n again, as many times as it takes. 'N by finding the right people to take advantage of."

"I know, but—"

"The council wants this, too. It be for the good of all of us. My time talking with you be up. The council comes now. We agreed that if you ain't already on your way to the docks by now, they could chase you off."

His father pointed at elders gathering outside, wearing council robes, prodders slapping loud and intimidating. The electrified ends sparked every time the Verkinn elders smacked the clubs against their palms. The flashes reflected in the growing puddles flooding the packed-earth roads. Three council members were joined by more, becoming twelve then twenty. All of that show of threat for him and sanctioned by his father.

Craze's reason ached from the whiplash of all the contradictions, all the switches from savage to tender. He couldn't sort out Bast's true feelings, and here he was suddenly branded an outcast among his own kind.

"They only raise prodders to chase off leechers

'n undesirables," he said. This had to be a nightmare. He banged his head on the bar. Pain flashed through his skull, white to vivid, consuming his senses, tasting sharp.

"Don't go getting hysterical about it," Bast said. "It's temporary. I told them it was the only way to get you to go, to brand you a leecher. They want the prosperity you'll send home. The rise of the Verkinn must come again." Bast's stance didn't soften, a snarl curled his lips. No matter the words, he wanted Craze gone. "All's you have to do is go out there 'n do what you do. When fortune strikes, which it will, the council will say you was on a secret mission for the Verkinn. A hero. A big hero, never a leecher at all. See, nothing to worry about. Unless you disobey me 'n the council's wishes. You to go, my boy. Now. No more arguing."

The words cracked like dried out branches in a windstorm. Bast held out his hand and Craze clasped the flesh as velvety as his own. Verkinn skin was soft as downy fur, irresistible to other races. But that wasn't why Craze couldn't bring himself to let go. He didn't want to leave Siegna or the village and everything he knew. He couldn't accept he would find another world and his place in it. As far as Craze was concerned, his place was here. With Yerness. What was up with her?

"Pa! I—"

"It'll take you forty minutes to get to the docks for the trip over to Elstwhere. They'll make sure you get there in time." He gestured out of the window at the antsy elders waving their electrified incentives, glowing like peril in the deepening dusk.

"We counting on you," Bast said. "Me. I'm

counting on you. I'm the one who said it had to be you. 'N just so you don't hear it from someone else, the council rose me in status last week. I'm permitted to take on 'n I intend to take advantage of my new rank. Yerness will be my second wife."

✦ *Chapter 2*

Craze jumped up off his stool. "What?" Yerness would marry his father? When did that happen?

She had said from the moment they'd met, she would only take on a mate of high rank. Rank Craze might have earned by now if the council and his pa had granted him his own ganya tree to grow his own business. It should have happened three years ago when he turned seventeen, but the elders kept saying resources wouldn't permit it. They just didn't want to share. Obviously neither did Bast.

Eventually, Craze's charms had softened Yerness's resolve. He promised he'd get the council to grant him a tree and believed he stood on the precipice of being authorized one. Attracted to his ambitions, she claimed she'd found joy in his arms. Didn't seem so now. Seemed she'd stuck with her goal to be wed to someone of higher caliber. That part didn't surprise him too much. But his pa? Craze's stomach pitched threatening to heave up all the malt he'd drank.

Crushed, he sank back on the barstool molded from a small ganya tree painted a festive red. "Why? Why her?"

"She was on the list of potentials 'n your ma likes her. No point in dwelling on it. What be done be done. Get along now. The elders is about to brand you a leecher. If you piss them off, they might not be so forgiving later. You don't want that 'n you ain't safe here no more." His father gestured at the council gathering outside, more than twenty of them now, brandishing prodders. "Get changed 'n get out."

Bast's features turned cold and brutish, his teeth showing in a display to emphasize Craze's degrading status. His father was suddenly a stranger, wheeling about and marching out of the bar, never glancing back, as if Craze were some drunk overstaying his welcome.

On top of the shocking news of losing his girl to his pa, Craze was to be branded a leecher. Seriously? He wasn't a Verkinn bum sucking off the success of others without putting in any effort of his own. He'd worked hard to help his father's tavern succeed. Slumping on the chair, he played with the empty crock between his hands, biting his lip to keep from screaming. Neither his pa nor Yerness were worth disgracing himself further.

"I'll never be so fooled again." He pounded his fist on the bar. The ganya tree quivered with Craze's latest assault, letting out an eerie whistle, protesting its continued mistreatment.

"Sorry." Craze rubbed over the spot he had smacked, smoothing over the insult. "None of this was your doin'. Was it mine?"

He raked over recent events and his behavior toward his father and Yerness. The only thing he'd been guilty of was trying to please them. His father had wanted more patrons coming in from other worlds, so Craze had spent time down at the docks selling servings of malt, sending the eager to the tavern when they clamored for more. Yerness had wanted a new dress, so Craze had saved his chips and bought it for her.

She should have said no. His father should have said thanks and shouldn't have been so chintzy with the chips, behaving as if the business hung on dire threads. Obviously it didn't if the council had raised his pa's status. Craze couldn't understand why Bast and the elders couldn't think of another way to get him off Siegna. A leecher? He was hardly that. His efforts in tending the family business had been double Bast's. Neither the measly startup fund, nor his lowered standing were fair rewards.

"Shit."

A scratch at the window made him start. Three councilmen glowered, their noses and prodders pressed on the damp glass. Their lips mouthed, "Leecher." The clubs sparked like fury, ready to chase Craze off as a village pariah. Worse than being torn to pieces, the humiliation of it burned, killing his dignity. If all Verkinn lost esteem for him, Craze might as well be dead.

"Shit 'n fifty times over."

He stood up and went over to the sad little canvas pack in the corner. Inside were a couple of shirts, the coveralls, and a photo of his family—Ma and Bast and his two sisters. He left the photo on the floor, letting his clothes fall on top of it as he stripped. His shirt and pants were rank and worn from a day's labor that had procured him no benefit other than lost love, lost family, a lost home, and the vilest label a Verkinn could acquire.

"That I didn't earn," Craze said.

He shook the pangs of injustice from his bared shoulders knotted from years of hefting kegs and sacks. The grievances wouldn't go. They fed on each other until a heat built, intense and scorching. He glared at the council outside. "I ain't no leecher."

Taking a fresh white shirt from the pack, he buttoned it up and put on the special coveralls made from a thick tan material. The new garments rubbed stiff against his skin, threatening to chafe. If not for the other bothers poking at his peace, he'd curse about it until his father apologized, which wouldn't happen. Bast never apologized.

The skimpy bag contained mostly belongings that didn't offer Craze much help at survival. Verkinn law stated his father could claim whatever Craze had earned while under his employ whether branded a leecher or not. Seemed Bast had done so and, judging from the sour-acting council, Craze couldn't count on help from anyone in the village, who were the only people outside his family he knew well enough to ask. To start a new life, he needed more then the meager few things in the travel pack.

He surveyed the tavern and the only home he'd ever known. Slipping behind the bar, he fingered the bottles and the curves of the ganya tree. Liquor held as much value as chips, so he put a few bottles in the canvas bag, and found some suspenders depicting a higher Verkinn rank. The council must have bestowed them to his pa.

The insignia of status could help from time to time, if anyone knew anything about Verkinn and cared. Craze cared. He put on the pair of red suspenders and threw the two others in his pack.

Rifling through a cupboard under the bar, he found a jar of ganya seeds. He took them, authorizing his rise into adulthood himself. No matter what the council and Bast said, he was owed this token of status. At twenty, he was past the time for it. His pa was right, it was time for Craze to make his way. He also grabbed some towels, tape, a spool of super-strong filament, and a lantern.

From another cabinet behind the bar, he scooped ricklits out of their cage into a smaller takeout carton. They were much tastier than the dried fish flakes from Elstwhere, or the processed grass curdles from Elstwhere's other inhabited moon. The bugs' iridescent yellow and blue bodies cheered Craze. Their chirping did, too. Rickl'ttt. Rickl'ttt. At least he'd eat well for a few days.

He still felt unprepared and intended to rummage about some more, but the council outside had lost patience. They bared their teeth against the window and smacked their electrified clubs against the sill. The chant of, "Leecher," rose in volume. Soon the whole village would hear and Craze would lose his dignity along with everything else. If that happened, there'd be no chance of coming back to Siegna ever, as no Verkinn would want anything to do with him. Once a leecher, always a leecher. He had to go.

Craze hoisted the sack over his shoulder and opened the door. The wet evening rushed in, slapping him full in the face with the feel and smell of Siegna, damp and mossy, earthy and mineral-sweet. He paused to savor a silent farewell with the tree and his home, until the council waved their weapons and advanced toward him.

Sparks arced from puddle to puddle, flashing over Craze's shoulder. He smelled the char.

"Leecher! Leecher!" Their voices shook the ganya limbs, surging up to the tree tops.

Shit.

Having no other choice, he set out toward the edge of the village. Hissing clubs and growling voices on his heels, he hurried past houses and shops constructed from ganya trees, lanterns glowing warmly in the windows. He stepped over tree limbs and through them, pushing vines out of his way. Youngsters swung on ganya strands above, chasing each other with shrieks of laughter. It was what Craze would be doing, were he not being run off.

The sway of the canopy roared softly in the breeze and summoned unbidden memories of Yerness in his arms so vivid he could taste her kiss. Hidden in a leafy nook, they'd basked in passion and lust, noses bumping, hands exploring, lost in the humid night panting and moaning, indulging in the feel of one another. She couldn't have meant any of it, and it kicked at him until all his thoughts filled with her torment.

The bite of fire rocketed up his spine. He spun about. A prodder had touched his ass and took aim again. Craze yelped. His pace must have slowed as he reminisced over the sweet moments of his now-tragic love. The pain of the electric shock swept Yerness from his mind and heart. He lurched, running, sprinting, racing until he left the village and entered the swamps.

"Damn bitches of Bast," he cursed the council between huffs. "Someday you'll all be sorry." He shook his fist and made several obscene gestures at the elders.

The thick bogs burped and splashed, covering Siegna's earth under millennia of muck. The coziness of the forest ended. The trees became fewer, spreading out with vast distances between them, giving way to grasses and sludge. Fish buzzed and gnawers swarmed without mercy while Croakmen harmonized with wild ricklits. The ricklit song spurred an interval of self-pity.

"No tellin' where I'll end up," Craze said. "Perhaps on a world without ricklits or anythin' much." The idea frightened him and he considered hiding out in the swamps. Who would know?

"Leecher," bellowed over the croaks and burps and buzzes. Brilliant fingers of electricity lit up the swamp. The council wouldn't let him hide.

Craze picked up the pace, following the trails through the wetlands. The elders persisted, wading through the muck, drawing nearer. Their electrified clubs whistled, sending out shocks in crackling arcs. Squishy things covered in hundreds of wiggly legs leapt screaming out of the bogs, their tentacles reaching to pass on their agony. Shit. Sting beasts.

✦ *Chapter 3*

Craze pulled three sting beasts off his back and swatted away four more. He rushed on toward the city and the docks.

At the outskirts of the urban limits of Siegna Landing, Craze slowed to a walking pace. He slipped between crowds of Backworlders and ground transports. The vehicle treads chewed up the earth and left soiled plumes in their wakes. Folks of a variety of Backworld races bustled down the noisy avenues, engineered canyons lined with businesses and homes.

Verkinn unaware of Craze's twist in circumstances waved cheerily. That warmed his heart some, until he detected councilmen in cloaks at every other corner brandishing prodders under the drape of their garments. They weren't shy about exposing the weapon tips to Craze's notice when he passed by.

Hunted. He didn't like it, needing no other

urging than being made to feel like an abomination to move toward the docks. Hurrying along, he vowed to travel far away, far enough away to forget this day. He hoped.

He trotted onward, heading toward the center of the city. The darkening skies were blocked out by lights blaring into the evening like a billion little suns. Gleaming beacons stretched on as far as Craze could see, highlighting facades great and humble. Buildings forged from alloy and reinforced ceramics spiraled taller than the ganya trees grew with the ones clustered nearest the docks towering highest. The shipping berths that rose above them pierced the sky, spreading out in welcome, lanterns calling in invitation to join the stars. The docking facility ascended like a teardrop, mushrooming out into a flattened sphere at the top where the spacecraft from Elstwhere landed and took off. Capsules rode up and down the sides of the facility as people came in and departed.

Craze stared at the elevators, his knees shivering. Once he entered the docks, there'd be no going back. He might never see Siegna, Yerness, or a ganya tree again. He wondered if his mother and sisters would wail. He hadn't been allowed to say good-bye to them. What would his father tell them? Craze hoped not that he'd been run off as a leecher or worse. Worse brought to mind several horrid races that dwelled out in the Backworlds, awful and despised. Craze didn't want to run into any of those, but he had no idea how to avoid them.

He'd never feel safe again. He knew that. His heart thudded and he glanced back toward the forest appearing so small from here. In the vast arm of the known galactic worlds, it was tinier than a speck. Specks were easily overlooked, and Craze was smaller than that. The village would lose its memory of him sooner than he'd forget them. The realization made him stumble.

People knocked into him on the street, rushing to unknowable destinations. He took pains to study the travelers, who were easily picked out from the others by their demeanor and dress. Wayfarers wore clothes many seasons out of fashion, appearing to belong nowhere and not claiming to be from anywhere. Yet their eyes shone bright as they ogled everything around them. Would he become like them? He couldn't imagine embracing other Backworlds with wonder. With him it'd be resentment, because the place wouldn't be Siegna.

He glanced down to compare his dress to the wayfarers. The shirt and coveralls seemed generic enough. His feet were wrong, however. Muck dried on his bare toes, and all the travelers he could see wore boots. "I can't go around the Backworlds like a Verkinn hick."

He took a detour among the shops of the trade district. Yellow and orange awnings set aglow by strings of lights fringing their edges snapped in the humid breeze. The aroma of roasting ricklits and the various spices used to flavor them filled the air. His stomach growled.

A display showing off the finest pair of boots he ever saw caught his attention. He stopped to finger the thickly woven fibers rubbed and oiled to gleaming. Their inky surfaces reflected the street and Craze's wide eyes. He stared at himself, seeing a face that matched his insides, harried and lost.

"Let it go," he whispered. "Get on with preparin'. Transport leaves soon."

He peered past his mirrored self to examine the goods more closely, searching for the price. He sucked in a breath. "You got rubies woven into these things?" he asked the shopkeeper.

The Croakman belted out a few bass notes, clearing his throat. He stood soft and wide, his jowls wiggling with his every twitch. "My sisters weave the finest boot cloth on all the Backworlds. You'll find no better. Not on Elstwhere. Not on anywhere. And they'll cost you more out there, too. Best bargain there is. Right there in your hands."

The merchant's jeweled fingers tapped on Craze's red suspenders, on the insignia showing his father's new rank. The Croakman's eyebrows rose and he sidled closer to Craze. "Those look brand new. A rise in rank means a rise in fortunes."

Not in Craze's case, but he didn't correct the Croakman. Craze's fortunes had been yanked out from under him, and he couldn't figure out how Bast could be so cold to his only son. However, any Verkinn would squawk about a rise in rank. Craze had to figure out a way to explain his odd behavior, and quickly. "You scammin' me?"

"No, my good Sir. Certainly not. Merely business. On such an auspicious occasion as this, I'll take twenty percent off. If we can come to an agreement?"

Twenty percent off was still a lot of chips, chips Craze needed to buy a new life. Taverns cost plenty. He probably didn't have enough to buy one. Positions in good bars weren't cheap either, but that was probably his best option. To get such a situation, he needed the boots.

"What kind of agreement, Croaker?"

"You see I sell other goods." The merchant waved his hand around at the shelves in his shop: neatly stacked bolts of cloth, trinkets crammed on tables and shelves, scarves fluttering on pegs from floor to ceiling, travel bags mounded into beckoning pyramids, luxurious clothing hung precisely on racks, and bling sparkling under glass. Things for folks with money. More money than Craze had.

"All very, very fine," the Croakman said.

A cloaked Verkinn councilman slinked by the shop window, pausing to leer at Craze, fogging up the pane, and pissing Craze off. Craze wasn't a sludge, wasn't a leech. He'd show them and Bast. He'd show them just like Bast had taught him, taking advantage where he could. The Croakman believed Craze was of higher status, presenting a situation to exploit.

Craze tugged on the suspenders, raising his chin. "Yes, I see."

"Well, my Verkinn Sir, you buy from me for the next year 'n that twenty percent off is yours."

Craze turned the boots around, examining them from all angles. They weren't glued together. Every stitch wove in and out the same as the next. With such exceptional workmanship, he'd never need another pair. He calculated the price versus the funds he'd been given to start over on another world. "Make it thirty-five percent off, 'n I agree."

"Twenty-five."

More Verkinn councilmen gathered outside the window, peeling back their cloaks to shake their prodders at Craze. They mouthed, "Leecher."

Craze bristled, silently cursing, "Assholes."

He didn't feel the least bit bad for what he was about to do. Time to take advantage of the swiped suspenders and take on the part the council should have granted him when raising his pa in status. "Thirty-three. I'm about to gain another wife." Damned Bast.

"Thirty-three it is then, Sir."

An elder with a prodder stepped into the shop. Two more joined him. The electrified clubs thumped against their palms in a steady rhythm.

Craze faced away from them, shaking the Croakman's hand. He gave over the tavern's payment codes to the merchant for the agreement presented on the tab—a slim rectangular card—binding his father to the terms. He grinned. Revenge did go down the gullet like fine malt. His thirst for it grew. He imagined becoming hugely successful on another world, the ultimate vengeance. A dram he vowed to sip at, betting it would be more quenching than this small nip.

Craze sat down and slid the boots on, lacing up the black chords strung through the thick black material that flexed like soft kid leather. He stood, admiring them in the mirrors around the shop. "They look good. Feel good, too."

The Croakman preened. "They look very fetching on you, Sir. A superb bit of business. What else you in need of?"

Craze could use a coat. He moved toward the racks. "Some outer—"

The councilmen grabbed him, shoving him out of the shop and into the streets. "Leecher, leecher."

Heat rose into Craze's face. He gulped. Disgraced enough for one day and not needing to be shamed in front of the whole of Siegna, he pulled away.

"I'm no criminal." He spat, jogging toward the docks. He would go on his own terms with his head held high, not be chased out. "I'm not Backworlder dregs."

He ran smack into two other councilmen with prodders. They pressed the weapons against Craze's sides. He screeched, his knees buckling. Sizzles jumped from nerve to nerve, making his skin burn. His head lolled and he lost his balance.

The elders took hold under Craze's arms, dragging him toward the docks, and screaming out his shame. "Leecher. Leecher."

Folks stared as Craze was hauled down the avenue. The Verkinn hadn't branded and ousted a leecher in more than two years. The spectacle had always attracted crowds of onlookers. This time proved no different. The day's humiliations piled up. Craze wanted to disappear, wished he were no longer a Verkinn.

"You don't want to miss your transport, son," a councilman said.

No, he didn't.

✦ *Chapter 4*

Dock workers strapped Craze into his seat as if he were some addled war veteran who never fully came home. Struggling to push them off and do for himself, he could only drool and grunt. He groaned loudly when an aviarman with spiky blue hair stepped on his foot.

"Sorry, mate," the aviarman said. His long sharp face came nose-to-nose with Craze's. He spoke to the other aviarman, one with red cresting his head. "I think we want different seats, Lepsi. There's something wrong with this guy." Movements jerky and darting, he tapped Craze's shoulder.

Craze's head lolled stupidly and he moaned.

"What's wrong with you?" the blue aviarman asked.

The aviarmen put their heads together, chittering excitedly. Their height was impressive, jagged and gangly. Jolting and stuttering, they stood close together, their sharp snouts almost touching.

Their mouths cut deeply into their faces, rigid dark gaps rapidly opening and closing, voices rising. The sleeves of their overcoats flapped, reminiscent of wings as their arms emphasized words with passion.

Their gray trousers had more patches than original material, threads unraveling at the hems, and old dust staining the knees. Threadbare khaki shirts poked out from under the brown coats, which were faded and shabby with buttons missing. Their boots sported more scuffs than shine, attesting to the many other worlds they'd tread. The aviarmen could help Craze by telling him about those places. If only he could speak.

"Conductor!" Lepsi with the red hair said. "We want to sit over there instead."

"You'll take your assigned seats," she said smooth as ganya bark. Her skin had a purple tint that clashed with the muddy green blouse, trousers, and cap marking her as the transport's conductor. "The shuttle is full."

"But..." The blue aviarman pointed at Craze. "That, Miss. Look at that. What's wrong with him? I don't want to catch a plague."

Alarm went up around them, whispers of disease and death filled the dingy white walls and rustled the faded blue seats. Something smacked into the back of Craze's chair, jerking him as if he rolled over rocks, making his lips flap against one another.

"There's no plague," the conductor said, placing her pointy thin arms on sharp hips. Her high cheeks and piercing eyes combined with her limbs hinted at aviarman genes in her family's history.

Craze had no idea which race the purple tint of her skin came from.

She flicked a limp curl off of Craze's nose. "He had a bit too much fun. Bachelor party his uncles said."

The aviarmen laughed, slapping their knees. They pushed at each other, joking, carrying on as if no one else had boarded the transport.

The blue one stopped abruptly, backing away from Craze. "Well, he could still vomit on us."

"Your seat," Lepsi said.

"The universe hates me." Moaning, the blue aviarman sat down and strapped in.

His friend stowed their well-used duffels, similar to Craze's, in an open locker at the wall separating the passengers from the crew. The reflective paint on the divider was worn and chipped, mirroring the travelers' faces in irregular patches.

"Hope you sober up before we get to Elstwhere, mate," the blue aviarman said. "Your bride over there?"

Craze groaned.

"You don't seem real happy about it." He shared the laugh with his buddy when the red-haired one returned and buckled in. "I've heard some about you Verkinn. Marriage has to be approved by the council of elders, right? So, maybe she's hideous? Loves someone else?"

Craze grunted, drool dribbling down his chin.

"Wow, you had a fantastic time. When you can, you'll have to tell me all about it. Seems Lepsi 'n I missed out."

"Did we?" Lepsi said. "Your nose often leads us into nasty alleys, Talos. Ones I can't ping to my brother in gloating triumph." He thrust out his tab with the image of another red-crested aviarman on it. "I want him to eat my dust. Eat it, Federoy," he said with a growl, before sliding the tab back into his shirt pocket.

"My nose led us to a ship." The blue aviarman, Talos, beamed at Craze. "I'm promoting myself to captain if it works out. No more spending a fortune going about on germ-infested transports. You'd better not have a plague, mate." His elbow jabbed at Lepsi. "Lots of bragging to send to your kiss-ass brother soon."

Lepsi danced in his seat singing, "Eat it, Federoy. Stupidest aviar boy. Damn to you, too, Kemmer."

"His father," Talos whispered to Craze. "Don't ever ask. Lepsi will go on 'n on about his nutty family for days."

The spacecraft rumbled, hissing. It jetted off the landing platform, drifting up and out. When it was far enough from the docks, the boosters engaged and the vessel lurched away from Siegna. Craze stared out the tiny slit of a window at the lights of the city growing smaller. They diminished into a clump, then a spot, then a spec, reducing Craze to a man from nowhere.

Siegna became the past, a former life which would forget him quicker than liftoff. A tear trickled down his cheek. The stun wore off enough to allow him to brush it dry. He straightened in his chair and stretched his jaw attempting to ask the aviarman about the ship and the places he'd been, but only, "Bwa wo bwa," came out. Craze's lips and tongue wouldn't cooperate, not fully free from the prodders' effects.

"Seems you excited him with your ship talk, Talos," Lepsi said, stretching his legs out into the aisle. "My family isn't that loony."

"Says you." Talos fingered a pin on the lapel of his coat, orange words with wings on a deep blue background. It said, "Carry on." From the twitchy corner of his eye, he studied Craze pointedly, on guard for plague probably. "His bride must really be atrocious. Perhaps he seeks escape."

Craze nodded.

"Well, I didn't buy the vessel yet," Talos said. "It may be a real clunker. But we can talk about it later. When I get it. You got a tab on you? I can ping you with where we'll be on Elstwhere when we know." He showed Craze his code.

Craze fumbled to get into his pocket and pulled out the slim rectangular tab, tapping a button to send his code to the aviarman's device. Talos saved it, filing it away in his contacts.

"You fwom Thiegna?" Craze asked.

Talos blinked rapidly, sweeping a hand through his shock of blue. "You asking me where I'm from? I couldn't make all that out, mate."

"Yeth."

"I'm from nowhere really. The aviars tried to settle on Doka, but we weren't welcome. Ended up scattering, everyone out for themselves. Lepsi 'n I teamed up looking for a new home. Elstwhere isn't it."

"Neither is Siegna," Lepsi said.

Talos tugged down the sleeves of his shirt, the cuffs stained and unraveling. He fingered the pin on his lapel. "Carry on. The ship will help us find one."

Judging from the clothing, the spacecraft would probably come apart as soon as anybody sneezed. Still, it was an advantage to exploit. If Craze charmed the aviarmen enough, maybe they'd let him tag along. He needed a new home, too, but he didn't say it. He couldn't speak about things he hadn't reconciled in his heart and mind.

Why had his father turned on him? The council obviously bought every line Bast had fed them. That explained them, but not his pa. Craze didn't think it could all be about one gal. Yerness glowed with dewy beauty, irresistible, but she didn't inspire traitorous devotion. Did she? Craze shook his head, watching reality in front of him change from a world he knew to one he didn't.

Siegna, lush and green, zoomed away. Elstwhere loomed ahead. Lusher and greener, dotted with great spans of blue, it was promising, as if a Verkinn could thrive as well there. The speculation drove Craze mad. There was no knowing for certain, not until he arrived. To ease his nerves and to forget about his ruined past, he mentally arranged bottles of booze by flavor, size, shape, and color. Orange with orange. Round with round. At first he rearranged Bast's shelves, then he moved onto imaginary shelves in a new bar, the one he dreamed to someday own.

✦ *Chapter 5*

The landing on Elstwhere went smoothly, just a small bump to mark docking with the berths in the main city. The conductor hurried Craze and the others off the transport, handing each passenger their bags at the exit. In thirty minutes the ship would take off for a more central planet.

Down the gangplank and through large arching doors, the travel port buzzed, thrumming with Backworlders Craze had never seen before—tall, squat, multi-limbed, no-limbed, invisible-skinned— the array made his head tilt. He had to catch himself on the nearest wall, chilled from the cold tumbling through the vents. Craze wished he'd taken another two minutes on Siegna with the Croakman to buy a coat.

"It's something, isn't it?" Talos said from behind Craze. "Elstwhere is always jumping. Ships coming in 'n taking off for everywhere. This is one of the best ports to come to when voyaging through the Lepper System, a main link between the inner and outer Backworlds. It'd take ten lifetimes to visit all the planets served by the Lepper. Then fifty more to visit those outside the system."

"I can't even imagine," Craze said.

"Come, I'll show you."

They proceeded down the corridor. The walls, floors, and ceiling of the docking station gleamed in gun metal. The aromas of grease and machine were overpowered by the stench of millions, an odor as wretched as the four-armed wench vomiting in the corner. Craze covered his wide nose with a hand, breathing in the reprieve of the ganya tree scent still on his skin.

The chatter of thousands of conversations didn't drown out the signals of incoming and outgoing vessels. Announcements blared at hurtful levels. To dull the commotion, Craze closed up his ear holes half way.

His adjustments to life off Siegna weren't through. The lack of thick organics in the air made him lightheaded. The new coveralls helped, but he needed time to acclimate to the garment's artificially produced organics. They tasted as though something was missing.

Shit. His whole life had suddenly gone missing. He couldn't lose the aviarmen and the possibility of passage on their ship. They might be his only shot at making a decent new life. Transports would drain his funds faster than the shopkeeper with the very fine wares on Siegna. He needed to plan his next move carefully.

He followed Lepsi and Talos to a wall with a

map of the portal system, the Lepper. Massive with thousands of dots highlighted in the Orion arm of the Milky Way, the chart caused Craze's wide-set eyes to cross. He had no idea where to begin, so he opted to exploit the aviarmen's greater knowledge. "Where you goin' next?"

Lepsi's head bobbed as he thought. "The planets closer to the Foreworlds is very populated. Not many opportunities left for those of us trying to make our way."

"Unless you have a mountain of chips. Real estate and positions cost a premium," Talos said.

Craze's shoulders sagged. "No."

"Elstwhere sits here on the border of the Edge, which is why it's such a popular port. The Edge," Lepsi said, his hand sweeping over the outermost portals, "is our best bet."

"Cheaper to go there?" Craze asked.

"No. Since there's not much out there, the risk is higher," Talos said. "That's the biggest drawback."

Craze took his hand away from his nose, adapting to the new smells and fewer organics buoying his equilibrium. "And the smaller drawbacks?"

"Not very hospitable describes a good number of the Backworlds on the Edge," Lepsi said. "Only a few kinds of Backworlders thrive in the extreme environments."

Craze didn't like the sound of that. He didn't want to know, but he had to ask. "Extreme?"

Talos jabbed Lepsi in the ribs with his pointy elbow. The gesture came off like a spasm. "You only speculating from stories we've heard. We don't really know, Lepsi. We don't really know, Craze."

Craze nodded, trying to take in the name of each port at the edges of the Backworld system. His finger brushed over a definitive and authoritative line at the leftmost boundary.

"Dividing line between the Backworlds 'n the Foreworlds," Talos said. "You don't want to go there, mate. Certain death."

"Certain?" Craze asked.

"The Fo'wo's claim we have no right to live. Kill us on sight."

"A truce has been called," Craze said.

"They don't care."

"Hmmph." Craze didn't give much credence to all the noise about the Foreworlders. They were just bogey stories to keep the division between the territories, so Craze believed. He knew the history.

In the voids between the worlds, the Foreworlds and Backworlds warred. Before all was lost for good, the Foreworlds declared a truce and named themselves the victors. The plans for their new fleet had leaked out, revealing the Backworlders had no chance. So the Backworlds accepted the treaty and the fact they had lost, scattering on the remaining Backworlds the Foreworlders hadn't seized. Making do. Adapting. Regrouping.

Craze traced the line, curious about where all Backworlders originated from, but he wasn't brave enough to face down the rumors. He'd leave that to somebody else.

Talos held out a hand. "Well, we off, mate. Carry on." He tugged at the lapel with the pin to emphasize the catch phrase.

Craze didn't want them to go, didn't want to be cut loose to flounder for the second time today. "What's that mean? The pin?"

The aviarmen stopped and faced Craze as if to shoo him away, but ended up staying put. Shifting their weight, wetting their lips, the hurry they'd been in dissipated.

"My mom gave it to me before she died. Complications from the war." Talos's lower lip quivered.

Talos didn't seem much older than Craze. Maybe aviar women were fertile well into life. "She was a veteran?" Craze asked.

Talos plucked the prized button off of his lapel, stroking its edges, caressing the words. "No, she lived on a borderworld as a child. The Fo'wo's let loose some plague. Made her weak the rest of her life. Not in mind though."

"Of course not." Complimenting the mother was obviously a way for Craze to charm his way into the aviarman's esteem. It was a lesson from his father Craze had often used. It stated that in order to get what's wanted, tell folks what they want to hear. Most of Bast's teachings wouldn't hurt Craze's prospects, but he wouldn't give the man any credit. It was Craze's ability to create the skills from the lectures that would serve him, and his many experiences in doing so.

Craze wanted the aviarmen to see him as a friend, to see evidence of it before they separated. Otherwise, he had no one and nothing. He couldn't stand the thought.

He wasn't above a little lying to manipulate the aviarmen's feelings and sway their sentiments. "I'm sorry to hear that." An untruth, because he had a hard time relating to affection for a parent at the moment.

"She was a great trader. As great as the members of the central guild until the recurring sickness forced her to give it up. I was still too young to be of use to her 'n the business. She gave me this 'n made me promise I'd get the trade route back, or a better one, when I was old enough." He held up the button. "Carry on."

"She sounds like quite a lady. What world were—"

"I've got to go see that ship, mate. For her. For the promise." Talos jammed the pin into his coat pocket, clutching it as if the fate of the universe depended on it. "When I get my trade route, I'll name the business for her." He turned to go, inching away.

Craze followed. "Nice. Won't be long once you get that ship. Then Lepsi can tell his brother to eat it, right? And, who else in your family?" He hoped that would stop them again.

Talos put a hand over Lepsi's mouth. "Condensed version: Lepsi's father favors his brother, Federoy. Federoy is an arrogant prick who can't put his shoes on right unless Daddy tells him. Go explore Elstwhere. We'll see you later."

They dove into the current of souls traipsing the crowded corridors, drifting away, disappearing among the throng of colorful Backworlders. Shit.

For a moment, Craze had an overwhelming urge to run after them. His mind reeled, unsettled, unmoored. He forced deep, even breaths while the coveralls squeezed his chest.

"Don't lose it now, jeez," he whispered. "A long way to go until this all resolves itself. Damn you, Bast."

Leaning against the wall, he soothed his nerves by picturing shelves and bottles in his mind, setting the containers of alcohol in a pleasing, precise order. His heart slowed and so did his pulse.

"It'll be all right. Will go find a coat 'n see what Elstwhere has to offer. Maybe I don't have to travel any farther than this." Right. He'd used his smarts to maneuver situations in his favor plenty of times on Siegna. There was no reason those same techniques shouldn't work on Elstwhere. All he had to do was find the right person. "Simple." Fortified, he left the wall, heading for the streets.

Verkinn elders dotted the station. He didn't detect any prodders, but he ducked out of their sights and into the sea of traveling folks. The asshole councilmen changed his mind about staying here though. He didn't want to settle too close to home and have to put up with their shit. Nope. He'd use his talents to get on the aviarmen's vessel and to make more chips, so he could leave Siegna and Elstwhere far behind.

✦ *Chapter 6*

Craze fought his way through the constant stream of people down to ground level and out into the streets of Elstwhere. He sought vulnerability to take advantage of, enumerating all of his past successes in increasing revenue for Bast's tavern. He knew he had what it took to make something happen. And he would. Dammitall.

He could see no end to the city. Its buildings spiraled to giddy heights, blocking out the world, most of the sky, and natural light. Many of the edifices rose to match the stature of the docking facility, sprawling in curling shapes, like a bizarre forest of giant dancers frozen in mid leaps and twirls.

He listened to unfamiliar languages, heard the squawk of traffic, and the shrill signals directing it. Doors slammed. People shouted and laughed. They pushed past him, rushing, kicking up the air that was dryer and more sour than Siegna's. He didn't taste as many nutrients in it. The coveralls were slow to compensate. His heart pumped harder, his blood flowed faster. His steps faltered.

People swore at him, shouting, "Dumbass." A couple of hard shoves sent him into traffic. Horns blared, treads churned toward him.

A hand pulled him back to the walkway. "You should be more careful."

The person stood slender and graceful, matching the architecture of the city, reminding Craze of new shoots on a ganya tree. He couldn't tell whether his rescuer was a he or a she, having purple-tinted skin and long dark waves framing a pair of flirty neon green eyes. As Craze watched, the Backworlder sprouted breasts which grew into an ample bosom. He had heard about bi-gendered folks, people who could change sexes, but he'd never seen it before.

A vine tattoo ran along her jaw line and down her throat. She took inventory of Craze, pausing on his new, shiny boots. Her enormous irises dilated, growing darker, and she licked her lips.

She saw Craze as prey. He could smell the predator on her. He also detected the possibility of profit. His pulse quickened at the thought of this game. The best thing was to let her label him as weak. He could use her underestimation of him against her, a vulnerability to exploit in the interests of business, the business of his own survival.

"Th-thanks," he said. "I appreciate you helpin' me out. This is my first travel away from home 'n I find this big city a bit of an overload."

Her face sparkled with his words. Craze could almost see her calculating what she could get off of him. The purple thing sniffed him. "I don't know your kind."

He didn't know hers either. The silver lamé of her romper stretched extra tight over all of her curves. She was dressed for distraction, and Craze could tell she was used to winning the way she didn't balk at meeting his eye. Well-traveled boots covered her calves up to her knees. He noted a weapon slid into the left one, then a blade resting on the inside of her thigh, just a quick flash.

"I'm Verkinn," he said, pointing at the Elstwhere sky. "From Siegna."

"Oh. Haven't been there yet. The Croakmen I met at the port threatened to eat me if I headed to Siegna." She cackled, a sound that matched the weaponry concealed by her flesh and leather.

Predator indeed. Craze needed to find out more about her. "Where you from?"

"I'm a Jix from Jix." She said it as if Craze should know.

Craze nodded. He wanted to come off as naive, not a moron. "Wasn't sure if all your kind stayed together."

"We do. Always." Her arm moved like a ganya vine in the evening breeze, snaking around Craze's shoulders. "You need a guide. Elstwhere can be a nest of bothers."

He pressed himself against her side. "I'd appreciate you showing me around." Maybe she wasn't the arrow to his new life, but Craze felt certain she'd point him at something that could get him what he needed.

She steered him down the avenues into a littered alley and into a seedy tavern. Smelling curdled and bitter, tasting of it too, the place didn't hint at any sense of ease when Craze walked inside.

✦ *Chapter 7*

Craze's feet stuck to the floor. With each step, he had to force himself free. Shit. He didn't want to ruin his new boots.

Murky lights, some no longer working, were set into the floor at irregular intervals, illuminating only black. Black rectangular tables and black chairs, the composite chipped and splintering. Black walls and floors. The tables had just enough space between them to squish by. Craze squeezed between four sets. Three more sat between him and the bar, making him feel caged and trapped. The Jix proved wily. He'd have to stay alert.

The patrons favored black, too—hats, shirts, pants, belts, scarves, coats, and footwear. Craze tugged at his bright red suspenders, very conscious of them, his crisp white shirt and honey-colored coveralls. At least his boots blended in. He clutched his tan duffel tight against his chest, following the Jix deeper into the lair. All the folks they passed leered at him as if he would sweat loot to be divvied up. The group was more odious than Bast's ambitions, and Craze knew the Jix aimed to intimidate him. If he didn't agree to what she wanted from him, he knew this crew would be used to get him to change his mind.

She waved at an empty table beside the bar. "Have a seat. I'll get us some ale."

Her hospitality, Craze knew, was to sweeten him toward her, to lure him into whatever trap she cast. He understood this manipulation. He'd executed it for Bast often. For now he'd play along, let her think she maneuvered him toward her goals.

He eased down into the chair, hard and cold, watching the shifty folks eyeing him. He fingered the tab in his pocket. The aviarmen were out there. He'd have to think how to use them to swing the situation around on this Jix. One thing he could do, he could ping Talos later. Maybe the aviars knew something about these purple gender-changing folks.

Dull ceiling lamps highlighted the bar and the mountain of a gal tending it. Craze had never seen such a wide-set woman and wondered what her kind was. The Jix slammed a cup down in front of him. She poured him some ale from a pitcher, then brought the ewer up to her mouth, tipping it straight down her throat, chugging more than half of the contents.

A putrid, chunky burp bellowed from her. She laughed, wiping the drips from her chin with the back of her hand, smearing the droplets of beer on her cheeks. "So, young chap from Siegna, you got a name?"

"Craze."

He sniffed at the brew. It smelled vinegary and weak. It'd be rude not to drink it though, and he needed her to think she had him where she wanted him. The beer tasted worse than it smelled and had bits of grain floating in it.

He did his best to keep his disgust out of his words. "What's yours?"

"Gattar." Her finger traced through a moisture ring on the table, drawing swirls and squiggles.

The shapes became more suggestive, phallic, and Craze mimicked the figures on his cup. No species had the advantage in the seduction game like the Verkinn. Once Gattar touched him, Craze would have her. He'd be in control.

The tabletop sported a sheen of stickiness. He wanted to gag, swallowing hard not to. Few races found vomit sexy.

"You just arrive on Elstwhere or you on your way out?" he asked.

She swigged more of the swill. "Just got in from a place out on the Edge. Bossilik. Know it?"

Craze rolled the liquid in the cup, but didn't dare take another drink. He didn't think he'd be able to keep it down. "No. Never heard of it. What's it like?"

She chewed on her lips, reddening them. "Fiery. Volcanoes going off all the time. Only one habitable island in all that chaos. Occupied by the Syliks. Know them?"

The rancid beer had a big bang. Already warmth flushed Craze's skin and his thoughts fuzzed, wandering. They landed on wondering how long the Jix would remain female. He didn't want to find himself satisfying the other gender later. Oh jeez. He should have thought of that much earlier.

He threw back half of his cup, getting the foul ale down his throat before he really tasted it. "No. Any around here?"

Gattar toyed with the zipper running straight down the center of her silver romper. "Haven't seen them anywhere but on Bossilik. They very dark with hard shells."

Craze let his eyes linger on her cleavage. As long as the Jix kept up those bosoms, he could handle carrying through with his plan to best her while she thought she had already bested him. "Shells?"

The Jix lowered the zipper, creating a deeper valley of flesh. "Yeah, like armor. When the volcanoes get to be too much, they curl up inside their own skin 'n wait it out."

He had to give her points for bringing up volcanoes. He stroked his cup, meeting Gattar's gaze. "Strange."

She traced the rim of the pitcher, picking up the droplets of ale, then sucked them off her finger. "Strange is often lucrative opportunity. Bossilik is a world very rich in gemstones. It's the only place fire rock comes from."

The action of her mouth tantalized him, but, ugh, she'd taste like that rotgut. And what if the Jix wasn't wholly female? This game grew ugly, but he had to at least see it through until he stepped out of this dump.

"Used in safe lanterns, right?" he said.

Her play halted, her hands slumping into her lap, eyelids narrowing. "Ah, you not as blank as you first come off. Not so fresh out of the Petri dish, huh?"

Craze grimaced. He'd messed up, revealing he might be more than she'd judged. Shit. He could recover. All he had to do was think of how he would know that and quickly. He went with the obvious. "Everyone knows about safe lanterns where I'm from. It's the only form of lightin' we use in our village. Good beer there. You'd like it."

Her frame relaxed, her fingers drew patterns on the table again. Phew.

"You a trader then?" he asked.

Her squint didn't waiver from him, scrutinizing his twitches and his lips as words formed. "Negotiator. A couple more good stops 'n I'll get promoted to captain."

Another transportation opportunity. Whether she bought his naive act or not, he could still seduce her, distract her. Gattar need only touch him once. He wondered if he could maintain feigned lust indefinitely to travel on her ship in search of fortunes. No, that would take more booze than he'd swiped from Bast or had the chips to purchase. He'd be better off with the aviarmen. With Gattar, it would be wisest to find out what he could and to get what he could before the next sunrise.

Craze moved his hand closer to hers, tapping the tabletop in invitation. "Wow. You must be very skilled 'n know a lot about the Backworlds." Flattery never hurt. "This is my first time off Siegna. Not sure I like it." Sincerity wouldn't be misplaced here either. "What kind of vessel will you captain?"

Her focus fell to his hands and stayed there.

"We Jix have our own ships. Transports mostly," Gattar said. "Certain sectors of the Edge fall under our jurisdiction."

"So, you part of the Backworld united government, the Assembled Authorities? That's impressive." Her choice of taverns was not.

"So to speak." Her mouth twitched and her legs stretched, brushing against his. Her delicate ankle rested against his thick one. "It's pretty wild out on the Edge."

"I think that's where I'm goin'. To seek riches." He extended his fingers to linger in the space between them, a proposition.

Gattar scooted closer. "Yeah? What kind of fortunes?"

Their point of mutual interest was broached and so started the real contest between them. Gattar didn't seem like the sharing type. Craze wasn't so much in the mood either.

"Business. Money," he said. "I want to own a tavern. A nice one. A destination."

She toyed with her zipper again; up and down, up and down, peek-a-boo with her bulging cleavage. "That's quite a dream. You ain't going back to Siegna then?"

Craze followed the motions of her zipper. The Jix was definitely open to seduction. Now he needed to find out whether she was capable of any sympathy. "Can't. The elders want to branch out. They chased me off."

The smile faded from her eyes and she quit playing with her zipper. "You their emissary? Your kind has aims on the Backworlds?"

The words snapped out like an attack of sting

beasts in the swamp. So, no. Empathy wasn't in the Jix's vernacular. Back to the art of conquest it was then. Whatever it took to hook into her avenues of commerce in the Backworlds, he would do.

Craze flexed his fingers, reaching toward hers, falling short in a beckoning dance. "Yup."

Gattar lurched forward in her seat, grabbing his wrist, squeezing and twisting until Craze winced. "Give up them thoughts, Crazy boy. The Jix be out here 'n we don't like sharing. You tell your hick friends that. OK?"

No, she definitely wasn't the sharing type. The threat worked in his favor, though. She'd finally touched him. Craze had her now, turning his hand and raking his fingertips gently against the inside of her forearm. "I'll tell them. Tell them my good friend Gattar is out here already negotiatin'. Negotiatin' for what?"

Her grip lessened and she pressed her flesh against his hand. "Opportunities." The Jix caressed his soft skin, delving her fingers into the plumper regions of his arm. "Ooo. Very lovely. Enhancement or yours?"

He flashed his dimples, tendering more of his charms. "Bequeathed to the Verkinn by the Fo'wo's."

"The Foreworlders came up with some imaginative improvements from time to time." She ran her hand up his arm, gripping around his bicep. "You strong, too. Huh?"

"No one on Siegna messes with the Verkinn." He flexed the muscle for her delight.

The Jix giggled, petting his flesh. "Very nice. The kind of nice that makes a gal a nice partner.

You interested in such opportunity?" She lifted the pitcher to make a toast, swinging it toward his cup, the smile suddenly dripping off her lips. "You not drinking your ale."

The stuff tasted as vile as Croakman piss, but Gattar seemed to like it, so he couldn't say that without offending her. He couldn't mess this up again, not when the Jix stood on the verge of falling for Craze's wiles. It didn't take him long to come up with another excuse. "Not craving beer at the moment." His lips pursed and he leaned in, stroking her wrist. "I'm interested. You find leads to fortune here?"

The Jix dumped his cup into the pitcher and finished the ale off, belching as she put the empty ewer down. Then she moved closer, her smelly breath inches from Craze's wide nose. "The perfect one should be arriving shortly. When I spied you, I had you in mind for this deal."

He tried not to inhale much, the reek of the house beer making him queasy. Despite that, he inched closer to her. Whatever racket she exploited on Elstwhere, he had interest, as long as she didn't prove to be a psychopath or worse. Craze didn't want to wind up in jail.

Gattar didn't seem as dubious as Bast though. No bloodlust sparked in her enormous eyes. So far. He hoped it would stay that way. If it didn't, well, he'd deal with the insanity then. This much he knew, the Jix wanted a rube for something and probably something quite risky to pluck at aid from a stranger. Risk meant great fortune. Fine. He'd play the part, and while doing so would figure out how to veer circumstances to his advantage.

Seducing her was merely exploiting a weakness, not a plan.

He breathed his words against her neck, watching goosebumps of pleasure rise on her skin. "What'd you have in mind?"

✦ *Chapter 8*

The sweep of the Jix's neck curved gracefully. She didn't push Craze away. In fact, Gattar moved her chair so she practically sat on top of him, encouraging his attention. He obliged, sliding an arm around her, flattening his palm against her stomach, splaying his fingers wide.

"So you need me in your negotiatin'?" he asked, using his experiences in scamming for Bast to keep the keen interest out of his tone and expression.

The rhythm of her breathing changed and she nestled in against his side. Craze suppressed an urge to gloat. She was putty in his hands, which meant more chips would be coming his way soon, and perhaps a heftier sum if he kept the Jix happy and purring.

"I need a big, strong man," Gattar said.

Ah, now she played him back. His potential fortune shrank again. For now he'd let her think she had him, to lure her in deeper.

"That takes no effort on my part," he said.

"Good." Her fingers curled over his, tracing the valleys and joints. Then she suddenly broke away, pushing his hands off and her chair back to its side of the table. "Go 'n get us more drink. Huh?" Gattar slid the empty pitcher at Craze.

From the corner of his eye he glanced behind him, noting three figures draped in black making their way toward the table he shared with the Jix. They swaggered, pushing around the rough bar patrons as they passed by them, flashing peeks of weaponry concealed in their clothing. The air became more fouled with trouble.

Shit. Craze could use a good nip to steel his nerves for the contest about to start, but he couldn't drink any more of that crappy beer. "Do you mind if I upgrade?" he asked the Jix.

"I still want ale 'n that's my favorite one." Her fingers drummed and her shoulders stiffened, ramping up her game to deal with the shadowy trio. Hardness stole over her features, a side Craze hadn't seen yet. Oily she was, oilier than a leaky valve. As quickly as her mettle showed, she tucked it away. With a big exhale, Gattar donned the smile of a coquette and blew Craze a kiss, giggling like a twit.

The change in her moods could disorient a whirligig. Craze knew he didn't want to be involved with her past one good transaction, which would put more chips in his fund. Nope. Beyond that would be utter foolishness.

The dark-clad people reinforced his decision. The kind of profit they might proffer, well, it had to be as shadowy as their clothes. Black market, illicit channels, secret trade, dripped off their hems like dew in the evenings on the ganya trees. They might as well have worn lit-up signs saying so on their heads.

Craze would have to be careful not to jump like a Croakman after freshly hatched ricklits. Eagerness would cost him in this venture. A mere percentage playing the Jix's patsy was hardly worth the risk. No, he wanted a bigger payoff and he knew if he could figure it out, the opportunity had just walked in.

For now, he followed Gattar's lead, playfully catching her kiss, holding it against his heart. "Ale it is for you, Sweets."

He only had to stand and take a half step to the left to lean over the bar and summon the barkeep. Placing Gattar's empty pitcher on the counter, he said, "Refill, please." He pulled out his tab, punching in the saloon's pay code that was painted several times in neon on the wall behind the bartender. "How much?"

"Two chips." The tank of a woman grabbed hold of the handle and settled the ewer under the nozzle, drawing the tap.

The beer gurgled out, glunking and sputtering in an uneven flow. Craze's stomach bucked, but he sent her the payment.

Head bent, he glanced sideways. The shady figures surrounded Gattar. She maneuvered her chair so her back faced none of them. She had some smarts. Craze couldn't deny that. He wasn't so sure about his own, standing deep in a den of cons slicker than Bast. He hoped his skills were up to this challenge.

"What you got in single malt?" he asked the barkeep.

She set two bottles on the bar. One would leech all the color off of the composites making up the furniture and fixtures in here. He pointed at the other in a round bottle that would still kick his belly, but it was at least drinkable.

"How much?" He hated paying for booze when better bottles lay in his bag, but it was rude to bring liquor to a bar. And in a place like this, it could get him stomped until he became part of the sticky crap on the floor.

The bartender set the full pitcher down before him, then patted the top of the malt. "Ten."

He nodded, considering the folks chatting with Gattar. Their clothes didn't have tears or patches. They weren't worn at all either. Along with the scent of trouble, Craze detected money. A lot of it. He hoped they were of a mind to share, and he would get the idea going by offering them some malt. It was a manipulation that had often worked for him on Siegna—give to get.

"Five cups with the bottle, please." He pinged tank woman the cost and a tip. Not tipping here would be as poor of a decision as drinking from the bottles in his pack, especially with opportunity so close.

He set the pitcher in front of Gattar and the bottle and cups in the center of the table, greeting the three folks in black with a thrust of his chin. Craze poured himself a hefty serving. It was a far cry from Bast's magic carpet, but steps above the rubbish the Jix drank. Then he gestured between the three strangers and the bottle. "Thirsty? There's a cup for you, too," he said to Gattar.

She shook her head, opening her throat, gulping down more of the house horror ale. That she could drink so much of it, like it, and not get sick baffled Craze. Perhaps it was one of the modifications her race's DNA had been given when it was spliced and diced up by the Foreworlders back on the fabled Earth.

He pulled at the smoky warmth in his cup, wincing at the sharp, bitter notes, notes that had no business in malt. The Jix and her shady friends had better make this up to him and his taste buds. Otherwise, this was the second worst hour of his life after the most recent one spent with Bast.

One of the gloom-clad things fidgeted, the drape of fabric rustling. "Yo still up for this, Gattar?" The words grated as if sifted through rocks.

So they knew each other and the Jix already knew what opportunity these mystery people offered. Craze wondered when he'd be let in on it.

The gravelly voice had to belong to a male. No telling what race of Backworlder he was though. Gravel Voice set a small bar, about the size of Craze's thumb, down on the table. It was wrapped in gold foil and a fancy red-gelatin casing that sealed in whatever it was. Such protection hinted at great value.

Gravel voice's thumb flicked in Craze's direction. "This yo new partner?"

Gattar arched her brows at Craze, indicating he should answer. Craze understood she had set him up, but he didn't know for what. Bending over, he tried to give himself more of the information he sought, sniffing at the wrapped bar on the table. The preservative casing held in any identifying scent, but he recognized the mark on the foil. He had seen it only once before in one of Bast's blown deals.

"Yes," he said without hesitation, because if that bar was part of a shipment of chocolate, he was about to become the richest Verkinn that ever lived.

✦ Chapter 9

Whispers from the underworld claimed chocolate only came from the Foreworlds, its origins still tied to the fairy-taled Earth. Craze didn't believe that, but he knew chocolate was rare and held dear, dearer than air and water on many worlds. Channeled through clandestine sources, the one bar on the table cost more than his entire startup fund. No matter what Gattar's intentions, Craze wanted to be involved in this trade.

"We partners," he said, moving to rub at the Jix's back, a show of solidarity.

"Then the deal is on," Gravel Voice said. "Yo know where we want to meet. Three hours before sunup."

Gattar nodded. "Agreed. See you then, friend."

Gravel Voice held out a small rod. The bar of chocolate floated up off of the sticky tabletop, attracted to the rod, clinging to it. The mystery man slid both objects into his pocket and glided toward the exit with his entourage.

The foil had to be magnetized to do that. Interesting. "Who is they?" Craze asked, sinking back down into his seat.

"Opportunity," Gattar said. "One we have to play perfectly. You need a lot of schooling might quick if we to pull this off."

Craze wasn't sure what they would be pulling off, but gave his consent. "OK. Let's get started."

"Not here." She stood up, draining the pitcher, setting it down, and wiping her mouth before she took her first step toward the door. Despite its inferior quality, Craze dumped the bottle of malt in his bag and followed.

His eyelids fluttered against the glare of daylight outside and he stumbled, bumping into Gattar. "Sorry." He donned a sheepish grin, wanting to grind home he was the rube she thought. He couldn't miss out on this deal.

The Jix considered him in silence, standing still. Craze didn't know what other factors she weighed other than she needed someone like him, someone fresh and strong with an intimidating build.

Gattar stepped into Craze's space, grabbing onto the front of his coveralls, tugging the material away from his skin. She peered down, running a hand down his abdomen. "You know what wealth they offer. I can tell you know."

It was the potential fortune more than the Jix tempting Craze. He didn't try to hide it, didn't pull away. "Chocolate," he whispered against her cheek. "Did you get to taste it?"

"No," she admitted.

"I hear it's silky." A good thing to bring up

while she touched him.

Those neon green irises grew as large as his hand and pierced through his calculations, stirring up pangs of guilt. He didn't know why, didn't know what there was to feel guilty about. A trait of her kind? Craze made note of the possibility.

"You can quit trying so hard," Gattar said, "I already decided to take you on."

Shit. It was what he wanted, then again he didn't. He feared what getting involved with her might mean, but he wanted this deal involving chocolate and would risk lying with something not entirely female to get it.

"Good." He backed her up against a grimy wall, tugging on that single zipper, aiming to find out before he lost all nerve.

Her chest heaved and she gasped. Her mouth was a little perfect O, enjoying his eagerness before she pushed him off, glancing at the busy avenue a block away at the end of the alley.

She wet her lips, but it was more a nervous twitch than sensual. "Fo'wo's be damned, no. Look we can't be seen together any longer out here. It'll ruin things."

He understood the paranoia with chocolate involved. No unnecessary risks. Craze was glad of the reprieve yet put on his best dejected pout, pocketing his hands. "Sure. If that's what you want."

Sauntering between broken bottles and crates, sashaying his hips, he headed for the main street. Gattar stopped him, tugging him back into the shadows, thrusting a tab into his meaty palm.

"Be there in four hours. Plenty of time to get

you ready." She let her hand run down the inside of his shirt again and pulled him in for a kiss, inhaling his tongue and his malt-scented breath. He was stuck with her sour taste from the swill, but the Jix knew how to use that mouth, which made up for it some.

As quick as the passion started, Gattar ended it. She took off, slinking and trotting, disappearing once she hit the end of the alley and maneuvered into the avenue.

✦ *Chapter 10*

Craze pulled one of the bottles he'd swiped from Bast out of his bag, swigging a good mouthful to get rid of the nasty tastes of inferior malt and rancid beer. No more than that, though. He didn't want to dull the excitement. Chocolate! More wealth than he could imagine, and he could imagine a lot.

How would he get the luxury goods out of Gattar's hands and wholly into his own? His first thought was to call Bast and the council, but he quickly discarded that. Their help would guarantee a successful sting, but they didn't deserve the honor. Instead he pinged the aviarmen he met on the transport.

"How's the ship buyin' goin'?" Craze asked when Talos answered.

A tiny head with spiky blue hair glowed in a corner of the tab's small screen. "We looking at it now," Talos said. "It needs some work to fly again."

"Can I come see?" A working spacecraft would go a long way toward getting the chocolate all to himself.

Talos pinged him the location and Craze made his way there. It was an abandoned hangar at the edge of the city surrounded by moldering warehouses and factories. Weeds wound their ways up the walls and over the walkways and roads. The pavement and structures crumbled. Craze kicked at the chunks, walking down the nearly deserted street bordered by chain-link fence, searching for the right gate. He pushed at entry 24357C, which screeched unwilling against the buckled tarmac.

Craze stood still, taking in the place, searching for motion and voices. He heard something in the direction of an old hangar, the roof sagging and groaning in the gentle breeze. The lot in front of it was littered with transports of all kinds: land, water, subterranean, air, and space.

A shock of blue hair bobbled above a flattened space transport. Shortly after, a crown of red appeared beside it. Craze waved at the aviars, shouting a hearty hello, greeting them as if long lost brothers.

"I can afford the ship," Talos said, "but not it 'n the propellant injector it needs to run."

A lime-green spacecraft, color chipping off the hull, sat on the rotting tarmac. It was a bizarre shape marrying six caterpillars ringing the center where a couple of beetles met back-to-back. Besides peeling, the green hull was pitted and dented. The hatch groaned when summoned open, threatening to stick or disobey altogether.

"How much does a propellant injector cost?" Craze asked. It'd be worth the investment if he could afford it. "How long to get it installed?"

"Lepsi 'n I could get the injector put in quick enough. It's only a two-hour job. The cheapest one is ten thousand chips. It's been hard used. Will get us out to the Edge 'n landed once. Then we'll need to find another to go anywhere else."

Ouch. That would spend most of Craze's startup fund, maybe leaving him enough for a coat and some basic supplies if he found a frugal shop.

"This one would be better." Talos pointed at another injector. "It's almost eleven thousand. Older, but not used as much 'n would last longer than the other. Probably has a hundred jumps 'n stops left in it."

A much wiser buy, but shit, barely enough left for a meal unless Craze bumped into a desperate wholesaler. He'd have to take the risk. Once he got his hands on the chocolate, he wouldn't have to worry about a budget ever again. "I think we could work somethin' out."

"Really?" Talos hopped from foot to foot, rubbing the pin his mother had given him. "Carry On."

"You about to get it good, Federoy," Lepsi said to his tab, his bother's image summoned to the screen. He started to sing. "A ship for chips. Give me your chips. Pretty, sheeny chips."

"Let's go talk about it." Craze shrugged a shoulder at an empty corner of the tarmac. "Away from ears 'n eyes not ours."

They climbed over treads and massive tires, ducked under hull frames and ship plates, then trudged over rubble and weeds until out in the open and alone.

"I fell into some business. So, I offer to finance the injector you need, if you can give me what I need," Craze said.

Talos took a step back, his eyes narrowing. "What is it you need from us, mate?"

"To get that vessel in workin' order by tonight 'n to keep tabs on me. When you get my signal, you come in 'n take up the cargo." Craze crossed his toes, hoping he'd judged the aviars as hungry as he was.

Talos chewed on his lower lip. "What kind of cargo?"

Just as he'd suspected some interest sparked there. Craze fed the aviarman a little more. "One that will afford you an armada. Your own transport line."

Talos stepped closer. "What?"

Craze whispered in Talos's ear, then Lepsi's. "Chocolate."

The aviarmen's eyes popped. Talos's tongue flicked at his lips several times, his fingers clutched over his prized pin.

"How'd you bump into that?" Talos asked

The hook sank in like a docking clamp on the aviars, holding tight to the lure of great wealth and a less difficult life. Craze breathed easier. "I met a Jix—"

"A Jix? Oh, shit. You can't trust a Jix, mate. Did you see the chocolate or did the Jix just say?"

"I saw it." Craze crossed his arms and squared his jaw, annoyed at the aviarman and afraid he'd made a big mistake teaming up with Gattar.

Talos chewed on his lower lip. "A plus, but still, a Jix is a Jix."

Craze needed all the information he could get. "You know about that race then?"

"Anyone who does any extensive traveling on the Edge or lives out there knows of the Jixes. They thugs who go about taking what they want from worlds that can't defend themselves 'n their assets."

Users. No better than pirates. Craze had thought so. "How many Jixes is there?" He had to know exactly what he was messing with.

Talos shrugged. "No one ever sees more than a few at a time. They have their own ships though. The implication is a whole population of them. Like in the old days before the war."

Craze would have to be extra careful then. Being hunted by the Verkinn was more than he could take. He didn't need other races ostracizing him, too, telling him where else he wasn't allowed to be.

"Ever hear of one named Gattar? She presented herself as a lass."

Talos's brows flew up and he whistled. "Shit. You mixed up with Gatt? A Jix with quite the reputation as a swindler. You won't get the best end of the bargain from her, mate. In fact, you should be thinking the shipment ain't chocolate."

Craze kicked at a vine. "Shit fifty times over. What should I be worried about?"

"Something more illegal."

Craze crossed his arms and drummed his fingers on his elbow. "Chocolate isn't illegal."

"Bet it was stolen. Either way, it's a great thing to use to cover up something that is very illegal."

The aviarman had a point. "Then we take the chocolate 'n leave the rest. Call the authorities in. Will help our getaway while the Jix jaws her way out of that mess. Brilliant."

Talos chuckled, apparently not opposed to wheeling and dealing. "Could work. Believe me, I want the chocolate as much as you do. We'll figure something out. Especially if we can find an Eptu or two."

"The Eptus? I don't know them."

"A lot like the Jixes, but they don't look anything like them. Where the Jixes be graceful, the Eptus be burly. They have big noses that can smell a lie 'n huge-ass ears than can hear an atom fart. I've seen the two bickering in saloons out on the Edge."

The Eptus could prove a useful diversion. "They don't like each other, huh?"

"Not at all. Rivals to the bitter end."

Very useful, indeed. "Finding one or two would be to our benefit."

"Leave that to Lepsi 'n me. Deal?" Talos offered his hand, his prized button "Carry On" cradled in the palm.

Craze had one condition. "All before nightfall."

"Speed is a trait of the aviars, mate."

"Faster than lightning, superior to Federoy," Lepsi sang. "Soon to be the richest sons of bitches in the Backworlds."

Craze took Talos's hand, then Lepsi's, shaking them. "Deal. Partners."

✦ *Chapter 11*

Craze headed back toward the central city, checking on the address Gattar had given him. The building rose eight stories, a ramshackle midrise of rented rooms squiggling left and right like a drunk, not too far from the seedy bar where she'd taken him earlier. It had been allowed to deteriorate, fading and dingy from the neglect of years, and Elstwhere's invasive vines threatened to reclaim it. Trash littered the stoop. The door sat half-open, stuck where it was by the buckling doorframe.

Craze circuited slowly around the block, noting the other businesses—pharmacies, bootlegged goods spread over cramped street corner stalls, diners, grungy mini-grocers, gambling parlors, and dancing girls. Other types of gals hung out in the shadows, trying to catch his attention. He brushed them off, branching out his surveillance to the adjacent blocks.

With his tab, he took photos and video, noting

the placement of security cameras and motion detectors. Craze wondered if the patrollers really kept track of it all, figuring they only reviewed images when there was call to do so. Would tonight create such a moment? He tugged at his suspenders, worried about exposing his face so much. Although, hiding it would perhaps bring attention sooner than he wanted. So, he kept on, playing tourist, stopping to look at products meant to part visitors from their funds.

"One of a kind Elstwhere plasticine. You'll be the envy of your friends on the central planets. Everyone will want an invitation to your place, to eat off your plasticine-ware." Not needing envy, Craze shuffled on, fingering scarves and knickknacks, scanning the side streets.

The Jix would want the meeting tonight to go off as low-key as possible. Those mystery people wouldn't want any notice either. Therefore, Craze figured the exchange might happen nearby. The Jix had only ventured to the docks for a rube, otherwise she seemed to prefer staying in this general vicinity. Craze could see why. The bustle was enough to hide in, yet not so much as to get in the way. It wasn't flagged as a notorious crime area. In fact, when Craze looked up the district on his tab, InfoCy said it was a good quarter of Elstwhere for families and shopping. Plus, it was close enough to the docks to make a ship useful and a getaway quick.

He enlarged his circuit by another block, keeping the location where he was to meet the Jix in the center. A row of wholesalers promising the lowest prices on Elstwhere led to an avenue with several abandoned storefronts. The street held promise as the place where the chocolate deal might go down. Craze noted fanned objects partially opened in front of the motion detectors on that road and boxy red modules attached under the security cameras, which hadn't been on the cameras on the other streets. Craze photographed them, relaying the data to the aviarmen.

Lepsi texted back, "Probably jammers to take the cameras off line or to loop them."

A thieving strategy older than the Backworlds. This had to be the street. Someone had prepped the area for covert activity. Who? The smugglers? The Jix? Chocolate was reason enough for precautions, but the tampering with cameras and motion detectors increased Craze's wariness.

He thought about what Talos had said about the Jixes and Gattar in particular, wondering what the chocolate might conceal. The worst thing he could imagine was a shipment of frizzers, taboo weapons of the Foreworlds outlawed on the Backworlds. If he planned for that kind of bad, he'd be ready for whatever the deal turned out to be. He hoped not frizzers. He didn't want to be involved with that, didn't like the idea of anyone on the Backworlds having those awful weapons. Setting one paralyzed the victim in searing agony. Setting two burned flesh in blue flames. Setting three calcified bone, dooming the victim to a slow, excruciating death. Taboo for very good reason.

"It doesn't have to be anything more than chocolates." A mantra to calm his worries, he said it again and again.

He ducked toward the most shadowed of the buildings, the one he'd choose for a clandestine operation he didn't want anyone noticing. Four stories high, a faded sign on its facade announced it as *Mr. Slade's Emporium*. Craze didn't know what that meant, what type of business Mr. Slade advertised. It didn't matter.

The sealed front door wouldn't budge. The caked-over windows revealed nothing of the inside. Craze went around to the back. Two doors were barred over and locked up tight. He tried them anyway. Neither had any give. The building next door had a half-broken entry. Craze slipped into it.

He crouched motionless, silent, listening, letting all his senses span out to detect anyone who might be there. The room he hunched in had been a kitchen abandoned in haste. Pots and pans, crates and cans, mud and dirt lay strewn everywhere. Smoke stains marked the walls.

After five minutes passed and nothing stirred, he crept toward the doorframe. He moved deeper into the building, seeking a way into Mr. Slade's Emporium. Nothing presented itself on the ground floor. Craze found the stairwell up and tiptoed over litter and shoes, old mattresses and discarded tabs. More tables and chairs filled an open expanse on the second floor. It was either more dining space or another restaurant. No doorways led to the emporium, but there was a balcony. A plank lay across its railing and rested on the sill of an open window of Mr. Slade's.

Craze crawled out on the boards, reaching for the sill, pulling himself over, pushing up the window, and letting himself inside. He huddled in the dim light, pressing himself against the wall while listening for activity within the building. The room he hunched in was stark and small, swept clean of litter unlike the restaurants he'd slunk through to get here. The difference was telling. This would be the place.

He heard nothing move, so he slinked toward the doorway. The next room was larger. Some shelves and racks with empty hangars spanned the space. It was obviously a shop in a former life. The exit yawned wide on the far side. Craze inched toward it. It opened onto a terrace ringing the interior. The expanse wasn't huge. Craze could touch the railing in front of the shop opposite if he stretched out his arms. He wasn't sure what it's purpose was. Perhaps to dress the goods up as fancy when the place sold stuff.

All rubbish and dirt had been cleared and banished to the corners. He glanced down at the empty lobby noting a large X and O marked on the floor in tape. Stairs led up and down. Craze went down, finding the entrances and exits, noting the crevices in which to hide.

He went back up, mapping any possible ways in and out on the upper floors, paying careful attention to anything that was something in all the emptiness. He spotted a pulley system attached to the third floor, set up with a huge hook and chains to handle the burden of heavy weight. A large metal disc topped it off. He touched it, sniffed it, observed an On switch. He flicked it, and the disc hummed. Clips, hangers, and wires flew up to slam against its flat surface.

"A magnet." Craze nodded, plucking off the

clips, hangers, and wires before shutting it off. He circled around the interior again. If this ended up being the place, he wanted to know it very well.

When done, he inched back over the boards to the building next door. From its balcony, he could leap onto the terrace of the shop across from it. He slipped inside the window and down the steps, finding himself in the backroom of a deli. Tiptoeing into the aisles, he was about to sneak out into the street undetected. His tab buzzed and he jumped.

The chime sent him in a hurry to examine the goods in front of him as if looking for just that very thing. He pretended to determine the best one, grabbed a jar of pickled snoink feet and tails, set it down on the counter, and hoped the shopkeeper hadn't noticed he'd ducked in from the back. It was possible. She was quite engrossed with her tab. Maybe watching a movie.

"Fifty chips," the merchant said, still giving more attention to her tab than Craze.

Shit. Fifty chips for something Craze wouldn't eat. Chips he couldn't afford. Not until he got his hands on that chocolate. Craze pinged the money over, glancing at the ID of the incoming call. He gulped. He should let it ring or cut it off, but the tiny face was one he hadn't learned to say no to yet. He wondered if he ever would.

"Hello, Yerness."

✦ *Chapter 12*

Craze left the deli, staring at the miniature depiction of his lost love. He hadn't changed her avatar, so hearts tumbled from her lips. Part of him didn't want to know what she had to say, but the part that did want to know won out.

"Baby," Yerness drawled. "You really miffed with me?" Her long lashes fluttered, each blink like a tumbler full of rancid ale in his gut.

"Shouldn't you be botherin' Bast? You punched in the wrong tab code," he said, gazing into store windows as he strolled down the street, acting as if he wasn't interested in her call.

"Don't be like that. It was the only way we could be closer. It was marry Bast or creepy old Confo. The elders wouldn't pair me with you. You don't meet my requirements."

She had known that when they met, ignoring his mid-level status in the end, toying with him all these months. His chest felt as if it sank. He rubbed at it. "How long you been aimin' at my pa?"

"Don't pout. It makes your lips all sexy. Wish I could kiss 'em up 'n make you feel better."

The kittenish tones raked over his nerves, rendering them raw and ragged, bringing on a case of tight jaw until he growled. "How long you been anglin' for Bast, Yerness? The whole time you with me?"

Her brow furrowed and the flirty smile flitted off her lips. "Noise of his rise was rumored in the council fifteen months ago. My uncle, one of the elders, gave me the list of potentials. I couldn't get stuck with Confo, Craze. Just couldn't."

She shuddered, scrunching up her pretty face, but her helpless act wouldn't work this time. His lips drew taut. "Your uncle 'n his friends branded me a leecher."

"Not forever, Baby. My uncle 'n Bast promise they'll get it lifted before the year is out, then herald you as hero when you make your fortune."

Those promises meant nothing. Bast and the council would do what was in their best interests like they always did. Craze didn't hold out hope for any other result. Unless he let them in on the chocolate. No, none of them deserved the show of respect. They'd only take it as a sign that Craze was a mark to be tromped on and used. Like he'd been under Bast all these years. He didn't want that. It was time to stand on his own, to rise above them and show them he was someone to take seriously. That included Yerness.

He didn't get this call. Although he now understood Yerness's motives in getting close to him, he didn't get what her current one for contacting him was. "What do you want from me?"

"We about to be family. Let's not be angry with each other."

What did she have to be angry with him about? He shook his head, stopping in front of a bright purple shop splattered with sparkles and splashes of cobalt blue, *Must Have Gear for the Edge*. Coats, bags, and supplies were crammed everywhere inside in no order Craze could discern.

"It doesn't matter," he answered. "We not allowed to be in touch anyway. Bast said. The council said."

"I know. Just wanted to call this once 'n say how sorry I am. Tell me you sorry, too."

She was something. Craze vowed not to let beauty play him like this ever again. "For what?"

"For not finding status 'n fortune faster, so I could be yours instead."

Craze sucked in a sharp breath. "I was on the list."

"Not at the level I need, Baby. Try to understand. You let me down."

He stepped inside the shop curious about what 'must haves' he didn't have for travelling around the Edge. The prices were reasonable and the workmanship of the goods not as shoddy as Craze expected.

"Look, I'm busy," he said.

She bit her lower lip in that adorable way, batting her eyelids, the long lashes sweeping over the lovely curve of her cheekbones. "Business already? I knew you'd do great. Just knew it. The sooner you make it, the sooner the council will renounce your leecher status. I can void my pairing with Bast 'n—"

"No, Yerness. You can take a flyin' leap off a space dock. I won't want you when I'm rich. We done."

He took their connection offline, deleting her avatar, blocking her code, grunting with a modicum of satisfaction. "Bitch."

The racks of gear beckoned to him. Craze rifled through the coats, searching for a dark gray duster in his size. A display of hourglasses sifting black sand gave him an idea. He splurged his last coins on gum, sacks of rice, and a patrol siren.

✦ *Chapter 13*

He met the aviarmen and gave them the siren, rice sacks, pickled snoink, and the spool of clear, super-strong filament he'd taken from Bast's tavern. Together they went over Craze's tab files from the surveillance of Mr. Slade's Emporium and the street.

Lepsi spent a lot of time studying the objects in front of the motion detectors near the abandoned emporium. "These fans will soon unfold so as to block the sensors," he said. "If we were to go back now, we'd see they'd be slightly bigger than when you were there. If they move slow enough, the detectors can't see them."

Craze peered over the aviarman's shoulder, reaching around Lepsi to scroll onto footage of Mr. Slade's Emporium. "I'm pretty sure that will be the place. It was neater than the other empty storefronts 'n it seemed arranged with the marks on the floor 'n the pulley system."

Lepsi leafed through more images of the emporium and neighboring buildings, slowing at the preparations Craze mentioned. "Most likely." The aviarman enlarged stills of the security cameras.

Craze placed a picture of an altered motion detector beside it on the tab's screen. "Does that look like the Jix's handy work?"

Lepsi cocked his head, considering. "My knowledge of the Jixes isn't that intimate yet."

"Shit." Craze's first-hand data about Gattar remained limited. It was an issue, but not a large enough one to prevent him from going forward. "That's about to change."

"Oh, yes." Lepsi chuckled. "We should know her very well by sunrise." He ran a hand through his shock of red hair, singing his concerns away. "Will we love Jixes tomorrow? Or will they suck like Federoy? Give me chocolates 'n I won't give a damn."

Craze waited for Lepsi to stop, his hair braiding itself into a single, thick plait down his back. He waved his hand over the rice sacks, spool of clear filament, jar of pickled snoink, and patrol siren. "Do you think you'll be set up in time?"

Lepsi nodded. "The ship is fixed 'n parked in a berth at the docks. We found the perfect hover scoot to borrow that can handle any crates of chocolate we find. We'll go work on that setup now." He gestured at the pile including the spool of filament and rice. "No worries, us 'n the scoot will be in place."

Craze rocked on his heels, tugging at his suspenders. "The Eptus? We still of a mind to use them?"

Lepsi grinned, slapping Talos on the back. "We'll take care of that, too. It'll be fun to rile them up."

Craze let out a slow breath. "In a few hours we could all end up very rich."

Talos held out his prized button, beaming. "Carry on! We'll be able to go far out on the Edge to places few have ever been. Find unique items 'n send them in to Elstwhere. A trade route of our own."

It was a dream as nice as Craze having his own tavern. Working with the aviars seemed a good fit, like the soft new boots he wore. He folded his new gray coat and placed it in his duffel. He handed his pack to Talos, giving more trust than he would normally dare.

A little voice warned him, "Remember Bast. Remember Bast." He told it to shut up. The aviars weren't Verkinn and they showed little sign of being totally despicable, just despicable enough. Like Craze. Like normal Backworlders. So he hoped.

✦ *Chapter 14*

The time approached when Craze was to meet Gattar. He entered the building with the half-open door. Rotting carpet curled up from the floor, peeling wallpaper in faded pink exposed crumbling gray walls, a sour odor permeated the dim corridors, and the structure groaned with each puff of breeze. Otherwise, the place remained as silent as a tavern at sunup. He labored up two flights of stairs, the treads worn unevenly from use, and knocked on the room number the Jix had given him.

She cracked the door, widening it just enough to yank him inside. "Good, you on time."

The room was no better than the hallway, harboring a forgotten past, an era before the war with the Foreworlds. Craze figured by the broken, splintering furniture, the building was at least that old. Shades of lackluster pink tinted the walls, floor, ceiling, and fixtures, like someone once had a fetish and no one ever dared to argue.

Craze squirmed out of Gattar's grasp, straightening his shirt. He handed her back the tab she'd given him in the alley earlier. "You said I have a lot to learn. Let's get to it."

He didn't want to renew their lustful play, not so brave at this point about discovering what exactly the Jix was under the silver romper. Besides, it was unnecessary. The Jix had gone too far to dissolve their agreement.

"I hope there'll be time for other things." Her lips brushed perilously close to his. "Depends on just how naive you is as to how long it'll take to teach you your part."

He'd act plenty stupid then, suddenly feeling the need for a bath. "I've never done anythin' like this before 'n I'm not exactly sure what this is we doin'."

"We moving goods. That's all. We pay the sellers, they give us the codes of the crates. We take the crates. I give you your cut 'n we go our separate ways."

The scenario worked for Craze, especially the last part. "What's my cut?"

"Twenty thousand chips. That's a whole lot of fortune."

Not enough to buy two bars of chocolate, and less than one percent of the haul. Awful pay. Craze bit his lip not to grumble. Gattar would be suspicious if he proved he knew the value of things. "Wow. So, what do I do?"

"We go to where the folks we met in the bar want to rendezvous. You go in with the chips 'n set the case on the floor. There'll be an X 'n an O. You put the money on the X 'n go back to the O."

Mr. Slade's Emporium was the meeting place then. No doubt remained. He'd deduced correctly, making him want to whoop at the top of his lungs. He swallowed the triumph, so as not to risk this chance at great riches. No telling when or if another would come along.

"You wait there," the Jix continued. "They'll take the money 'n put down some crates. A few moments later, they'll give you the codes. We test them, check the goods, then we move the crates. I pay you. You go away."

Craze sure hoped Lepsi and Talos would have everything ready in time, and he hoped they wouldn't double cross him. Nah, they were too grateful for the propellant injector for their ship. They'd made him crew. They'd be true to their word. So Craze kept telling himself. "Doesn't sound too complicated."

"But if you do it wrong, they'll shoot you."

There was the rub. He'd be the one on the firing line. "I see."

"Still up for this?"

"Twenty thousand is a lot of chips." Craze grinned as if the amount really excited him. In a way it did. It was more than Bast had given him. "So, yes."

"Good."

Gattar sauntered close, running her fingers over his chest, getting too friendly, reaching for his exposed skin. Craze really didn't want to go there with the Jix. Really, really didn't want to. He twisted and wiggled to keep her touch on his clothes, checking the hour on a pink clock on a tilting table. Three and a half hours until the rendezvous, an eternity to do what she hinted at, and several times over at a languid pace. Shit.

"Show me again exactly how to walk into the place 'n hold the case of chips. I don't want to get shot." Normally, he hated acting so stupid, but not in this situation.

✦ Chapter 15

At an hour when the city lay motionless, poised in suspension until the sun rose again, Craze stood inside Mr. Slade's Emporium. The front door was now unsealed, and a case filled with chips was in his hand. The money weighed a lot, threatening to make him walk lopsided. He resisted, striving to regain the dignity Bast and the council had robbed him of on Siegna.

He set the burdened attaché down on the enormous X on the floor. Nothing in the lobby had changed from his earlier visit except for the sacks of rice piled beside some trash on a shelf. Craze noted a piece of vine beside the sacks, a signal from the aviarmen that the clear filament was attached, holding the jar of pickled snoink at the fourth floor above the magnet and pulley system the smugglers had installed. He chanced glancing up, relieved not to see the shine of glass from the jar. The aviars must have painted it black as they had planned.

Although he was glad to know Talos and Lepsi had everything in place, Craze's shoulders didn't unclench and his steps came off stiff as he lumbered to the O taped out a good twenty feet away. He stood mute in its center. A low hum disturbed the heavy quiet. The case shot up. A loud clang thundered through the empty building.

The magnet. Craze looked up, studying every shadow for movement, but he couldn't detect the mystery folks. There had to be at least one above him to get the attaché of chips off the powerful magnet. Where were the others and how many? Another wild card in tonight's scheme. He opened his ears wide to learn all he could, hoping the aviars had discovered more intel on the smugglers.

Another clunk disturbed the darkness. The hum stopped, replaced by the roaring engine of a generator. The pulleys lurched, squeaking as they turned. Craze spied a cube swinging above him. Light leaking in from the lamps outside weakly glinted off the large hook and chains. Gyrating like a pendulum, a pallet of crates groaned toward the floor, landing with a solid thunk.

As commanded by the smugglers, Craze kept his hands visible and his mouth shut. He stretched his fingers wide apart, knowing the aviarmen watched for his signals, subtle motions they'd worked out earlier.

Excitement trembled through Craze's knees as he approached the pallet. His fingers shook unhooking it from the line that had lowered it. The symbols on the crates were strange, not anything Craze had seen before. A white circle with four thick red lines. He'd heard about it though. It marked the Foreworlds.

Shit. The worse situation he'd imagined could be possible. Like chocolate, frizzers only came from the Foreworlds. Backworlders wouldn't touch the cruel weapons that burned the skin and calcified bone. Horrid, horrid things. It bothered him that some Backworlders wanted those guns, and would stoop to using them. That went beyond dastardly to traitorous.

He wanted to signal the aviarmen now, his first two fingers snuggled tight against his thumbs, to call in the authorities, but it was too soon. The smugglers hadn't sent the codes. He hadn't gotten his hands on the chocolate. He desperately needed a return on his investments in this venture. Just one sack full of chocolate would help him and the aviars establish a great life out on the Edge.

Codes flashed in light on the floor. Craze punched the icons and numbers into the keypad on the first crate. The carton slid open with a soft whoosh. He placed the gum from his mouth over the latching mechanism to prevent it from resealing. The door opened and shut in a loop as it hit the sticky obstruction. Craze wiggled his left index and middle fingers for the aviarmen. The response came almost instantly.

Eptus streamed in from above, where they'd been hiding on the fourth floor. Square torsos with powerful limbs, they moved more agilely than their frames suggested. Enormous ears pivoted on their heads, which were canine in nature. So were their noses. Barking and shooting flash guns, they descended into Mr. Slade's Emporium.

Craze covered his eyes against the blinding weapon fire. Stumbling, he grabbed onto the crate for balance. He missed. His hand sank into the chocolates, coming up with a frizzer. Craze yelped. The Eptus shot all around him, too close to be trusted. He dropped the forbidden gun and ran toward the shelf with the rice, slashing at the sacks with his fingernails.

The grains spilled out, falling to the floor as they depleted the sacks of their ballast in a rush. The bags lightened, and the jar of pickled snoink pulled them up off the shelf. The jar sank until the heavy glass hit the magnet switch and broke with a crack then a tinkle. Blackened shards, feet and tails, and pickle juice rained down, inciting the Eptus into a rage. They fought each other to snap up the brined morsels, grabbing, shoving, biting, swallowing without chewing.

The chocolates flew up, their metal foil wrappings attracted to the magnetic field. The layer of chocolate bars was thinner than Craze would have liked, but as few as thirty bars would allow him to recover the money he had spent and make a decent profit to share with Talos and Lepsi.

While the Eptus busied themselves vying for pickled feet and tails, Craze scrambled for the stairs. Two people draped in black stood under the pulley system holding a bag under the magnet. They turned off the power, chocolates dropped into their sack. The dark figures snatched up the few bars that escaped onto the floor, then their palms faced Craze, open and pale. They clenched their hands into fists three times before running down to the second floor and into the deep shadows. Craze sure hoped the chocolate takers were Talos and Lepsi. Their signals said so, but their mimicking of the smugglers was spot-on enough to stir up doubt.

He chased after them, his coveralls working hard, his lungs laboring in air not as enriched as Siegna's. Eyelids fluttering and thoughts slowing down, his body threatened to hibernate. To avoid it, he had to slacken his pace, letting the distance between him and the chocolate grow. It worked, his lungs filled more easily and he no longer felt an overwhelming urge to sleep.

Seven seconds later, the patrol siren blasted through Mr. Slade's Emporium. Much too early. They hadn't made it out of the building yet. Craze shouted at the aviars, gesturing wildly to cut the blaring horn. They didn't hear and didn't see, racing toward the room with the window leading to the balcony next door.

Craze sprinted after them, a good twenty feet behind. He leapt out of the window and onto the plank, shimmying over to the restaurant terrace. About to jump over to the deli, he was stopped in mid-air. Three pairs of hands pulled him back, then inside the abandoned diner, handcuffing him to a pipe.

Several badges flashed past Craze. Blinking red and blue lights joined the sirens. The earlier alarm hadn't come from the toy Craze purchased at *Must Have Gear for the Edge*. It had come from real patrollers. Swarms of them swathed in lime green.

The brightly colored uniforms ran past him, intent on Mr. Slade's Emporium, pouring through every door and window, raiding the failed deal.

Eptus howled. Amplified patroller voices barked orders. Craze wondered about Gattar and the mystery folks in black. Had they gotten away? He doubted the Jix would pay him now and tugged at his binds. They and the pipe held solid. Shit.

✦ Chapter 16

Five patrollers swaggered up to Craze when the noise died down. They freed him from the pipe, herded him downstairs and over to Mr. Slade's, jabbing and shoving until Craze was surrounded by Eptus. Some of them growled, low and steadfast, giving Craze a headache. He didn't see the aviars, the Jix, or the people in black.

All of the crates were upended. Patrollers quickly counted and secured the frizzers, glaring at Craze and the Eptus as they did. The only worse crimes than possessing frizzers on the Backworlds were using them, and betraying fellow Backworlders to the Foreworlders.

Craze was pissed the Jix had left him to deal with the authorities alone, but relieved the aviars got away. Part of him clung to a small hope they'd come after him and break him out of patroller custody, but dammitall, if his own father had abandoned him, then a couple of dudes who were little better than strangers probably would, too. He'd have to get out of this mess using his wits, and watched his opportunity approach.

A group of squat patrollers swaggered across Mr. Slade's lobby and came to stand before Craze. None of them rose higher than four foot six inches. They all had wide, powerful frames, and long silky hair. All but one of the six were dressed in green. The oddball wore brown, layers and layers of brown.

The lead patroller sniffed at Craze. "You Verkinn nutty. I don't like when you come over here. You best stay over on Siegna."

Great idea. "I'd be happy to leave." Craze doubted escape would be so easy.

The patroller put his hands on his hips, pursing his lips. "This is serious trouble, boy."

Nope, freedom wouldn't come simply. Craze resisted sighing, concentrating on the patroller's words, seeking an opening to poke wider that would land him at the docks and on the aviarmen's ship.

The lawman jabbered on. "This wasn't some small scam taking a few chips off a citizen, this crime threatens all the Backworlds. The Assembled Authorities have been notified. Frizzers bad news."

Shit. "I didn't know it was frizzers." Craze had to try some truth. "You better have found every one of those guns. I don't ever want to run into one of them things out on the Edge. I wouldn't touch the things. Honest. I was here for the chocolate."

"There's no chocolate here," the patroller said.

"The bars. The foil bars." Craze thrust his chin

toward the small red and gold items strewn over the floor.

The lawman picked one up. "These?" His small, meaty hands unwrapped the bar, holding it out under Craze's wide nose. "Mealworm cakes, son. That's all these is."

Craze smelled the brine, gawking at the red crumbly cake in the patroller's hand. That couldn't be right. That couldn't be what was protected by the foils and gelatin casings. The seal… the seal embossed on the foils was used for chocolates. Yet he couldn't argue with the reality in front of his face.

His breath suddenly left him. "No!"

The squat man in brown laughed. "He didn't know. He honestly thought he was buying chocolate."

The patrollers joined in the mocking. The leader said. "Verkinn sure can be gullible. Guess the aviars was right then." He shook a finger at Craze. "Deal through legit channels, boy, 'n only from folks you know. This clandestine shit only leads to bothers."

Sometimes to great profits, but Craze kept that to himself. The aviars had to be Talos and Lepsi. Phew. They hadn't abandoned him to battle these legal woes in order to get a bigger cut of the loot. Despite being cuffed by the patrollers and probably on his way to prison, Craze felt pretty good.

He regained some sense of belonging, which Bast and the council had stolen by ostracizing him. Things would be OK. He had two good friends. Craze knew that without a doubt, and he also knew the patrollers didn't think him very bright. He'd use that. "I never tasted chocolate before. Just wanted to see what all the fuss is about."

"That's what your captain said. Said you often a dipshit," the patroller replied.

"Cappy's never wrong." Craze was impressed by the aviarmen's skill at manipulating the legal authorities.

"You not getting off easy, you understand." The lawman nodded, satisfied and smug. "Your captain is pretty hot, promised us you'd help in chasing after these thugs. After he's punished you."

"I'm sure. The brig for me." Craze enjoyed playing along, careful not to go too far and blow what Talos and Lepsi had accomplished, wondering how he was supposed to assist the Elstwhere law, but he didn't press. Sooner or later he'd know everything.

"The Backworld Assembled Authorities gave me the OK to track these barbarians down," the man in brown said. He grabbed Craze's wrist, tugging him onto his feet. "I'll see he finds his way to his ship. Consider youself deputized, Verkinn."

Deputized? A funny thought came to Craze. The aviars' promises, the Backworlds Assembled Authorities' approval, being deputized; perhaps Talos and Lepsi's ship had been hired to pursue the smugglers. Shit. The reach of the law was long if it was to follow them out to the Edge.

The patroller leader nodded. "All right, Dactyl. You'll find half the agreed on pay in your account when you get to the docks. If not, ping me."

"I expect the rest when I haul those smugglers back here for interrogation 'n trial," Dactyl said.

"Good hunting." The patroller saluted. "We want that scum. Want them bad. Get in contact if you need anything from us."

Dactyl nodded. His iron grip tightened on Craze's shackles, dragging him out into the street and toward the docks. He led Craze in such a way that folks stopped gape-jawed, pointing and whispering.

Craze became a spectacle of shame paraded off Elstwhere, not so different from how he left Siegna. Shit. "This is gettin' to be a pattern," he said.

✦ *Chapter 17*

The ship looked sad in the well-maintained dock, hideous and long past its prime. It was an awful shade of green, chipping and peeling. And it was shaped so odd, like two beetles back to back with six cylindrical protrusions sticking out from the center that reminded Craze of worms.

He seriously questioned his sanity. Wow. That was what he would travel the Backworlds in? That was what he invested most of his chips on?

Dactyl shoved Craze forward onto the boarding ramp and into the hatch at the end of one of the worm-like extensions. Once on board, the lawman released Craze's hands from the binds. "Yous watch youself. The patrollers told me to keep yous on probation. One wrong move 'n yous to jail."

Around the bend, the aviarmen stooped side by side. The confines of the entry made them appear taller than usual, creating the unmistakable impression that they owned this spacecraft. They wore serious airs, furrowing their brows, and burying their hands deep in their coat pockets. The similarity of their dress and stance gave them the guise of a uniformed crew, which made Craze feel a little left out. Although he wore mostly browns and grays too, it was in a different order and his boots were still shiny. It was of minor consequence though, as he was incredibly relieved to be back at the docks with the aviars.

Craze rubbed at the chafing left as a memento by the cuffs, grinning at Talos and Lepsi. "Thanks." He raised his brows in Dactyl's direction wondering how the patroller planned to enforce the probation. Then a horrible possibility crept to mind. Was Dactyl going with them? Craze tried to relay the question to the aviarmen through his expression.

Talos's tentative smile and tug on his prized pin, signaled their carefully crafted exit strategy had changed. "Welcome back, Second Officer Craze." He ran a hand through his shock of blue. "Before you join us on the bridge, the Sequi could use a good cleaning." From behind his back he brought out a bucket full of cleaning gel and some clothes.

"The Sequi?" Craze asked.

"The Backworld Assembled Authorities granted our ship the honorable name when we was deputized."

Did that mean Dactyl was or wasn't remaining on board? Craze clenched his jaw, wishing the lawman away. It'd be about impossible to recover his lost investment with a patroller on board.

Talos kept talking. "The Authorities is short on ships 'n since we saw the vessel the frizzer runners left in, we agreed to help out Dactyl in apprehending those despicable infiltrators."

Translation: the lawman would stay and the aviarmen had seen the smugglers' ship. They'd told the Authorities. The only reason to do so was to get Craze sprung. Ah, he'd prove they'd made the right decision and not screw this up. What a beautiful thing they'd engineered—thieves chasing after smugglers. Craze had to bite the inside of his cheek to keep from laughing. He peered into the yellow slop, doing his best to remain somber. "Yes, Sir."

"No more dipshit behavior, Second. I need my crew if I'm to chase those criminals down effectively. The Authorities agreed as long as I saw to it you was punished."

The aviars must have emphasized Craze's skills as essential to get the Authorities not to insist Talos hire a new crewman. Warmth spread in his chest and dimpled his cheeks. Craze saluted the aviarmen, fist to chest. "Yes, Captain."

Talos clasped his hands behind his back, standing straighter. "Clean every inch of this ship 'n don't be all day about it. If you do unsatisfactory work, I'll have to withhold your pay."

Pay? Maybe something could be salvaged out of this mess. Impatience to know more threatened to do Craze in. He gripped the bucket handle tight, squeezing until the urge lessened into something he could control. "Understood, Sir."

"Carry on, Second." With a curt nod, Talos stepped down the corridor toward the center of the spacecraft. Lepsi and Dactyl followed.

Craze began his atonement at the hatch and the

pressure lock. The passageway was an aging emerald green except in the spots where the reinforced carbon composite had worn. In those places, the ship was a dingy white. Gray lockers for eight crew members lined the entryway. Four of them contained spacesuits and helmets. On closer inspection, only one of the suits actually functioned. Great.

Craze moved on. The passage led to a living area the size of an efficiency. If everyone on the Sequi hung out in here, they'd be tripping over each other, and forced into each other's faces. It'd be all the worse with a full complement on board. What if the aviars hired more crew?

Craze's vision shivered. His knees soon followed. Dammitall. The walls sensed his fear, creeping in, eating up valuable inches. Oh jeez. He pushed at them, suspecting he might not be cut out for space travel. For the time being, however, he was stuck with it as his way of life. At least until he found a place to settle. He hoped that wouldn't take too long.

Whether it took twelve minutes or years, he needed to calm down. With determination normally reserved for scamming chips from rubes, he forced his terror into the background, imagining the tavern he would someday own, rearranging the bottles on the shelves. Gin with gin. Low quality to high. Ouzo with ouzo. Biting to flavorful. The panic faded. He took a deep breath. The Sequi reeked, rank as old shoes in a filthy barn.

Leaving the wall, he continued cleaning, expunging the grunge settled over everything in the common living space. The composite gleamed in a paler green, glossy as glass when he applied the gel. He noticed other things besides the lack of room now. Ladders in the center led up and down. Five other corridors besides the entry branched off the walls, their doorways almost flush with the living compartment. Craze peeked in one. Crew quarters.

He scrubbed the floor and the kitchenette, which was no bigger than a closet, and wiped down the table, chairs, and exercise equipment. Covered portholes were placed between the entries to the private compartments. He unhinged them and cleared each pane of smudges.

Before he finished with the windows, the ship boomed to life, vibrating with energy, enthused to get going. Craze stayed at the last porthole he had cleaned, watching as the Sequi zoomed away from Elstwhere, the planet and Siegna shrinking as the distance grew. Up ahead, cobalt burst into the heavens like a new star being born. The light opened up to reveal the portal of the Lepper System. With a small shudder, the Sequi slipped inside. The stars and planets disappeared behind the corridor of blue light, leading onward or maybe backward. It was hard to tell.

Craze next straightened and dusted the crew quarters branching off of the living area. Three rooms had only one bunk, the others had two sleeping spaces inside. In one of the singles, he found his pack set on a comfortable bed. He smiled at the aviarmen's continuing thoughtfulness, once again grateful he'd bumped into them on the transport from Siegna. Some drawers and a fold-down desk completed the furnishings.

After sprucing up the residential spaces, Craze

climbed down the ladder and worked over engineering and the storage bays with the cleansing gel and rags. When he finished, he climbed the ladders up to the bridge where he found Talos, Lepsi, and Dactyl.

He longed to ask the aviars about the chocolate, possible pay, and everything else. Did they nab any chocolate or was it all mealworms? He couldn't, not with the extension of the Elstwhere patrollers sitting there. He couldn't believe they ventured out to the Edge with a representative of the Backworld Assembled Authorities on board. It would definitely crimp Craze's style. He'd have to go after his dream above-board and honest. He feared such behavior would keep him poor.

Dactyl had removed several layers of brown, but he was still very brown. What he lacked in height, he made up for with an aura of intimidation clinging to his shoulders and close-shaven beard. His eyes were the color of tree bark and his hair a reddish shade, but it was still mostly brown. It waved down past his waist, neat and gleaming. Since it wasn't living, he must have spent a lot of time caring for it.

Craze felt his hair coiling itself into neat rows in response, brushing against his shoulders. He cleaned the bridge, dousing things in gel, then wiping them off with the cloths. The mustiness of the aged Sequi lessened, infused with the fresher scent of citrus. When all gleamed spotless, Craze took the bucket and rags down to a storage closet. Then he climbed back up to the bridge and took a seat.

An island of console and systems took up the

center of the bridge in a circular shape. Talos was in the central command position, Lepsi sat on his right. Dactyl had assumed a crew station behind the two of them. Craze chose the position on Talos's left. Large windows banked the walls with wide glimpses outside, providing close to a three hundred sixty degree view. Blue. All he saw was blue.

"Do we have a plan?" Craze asked.

Talos answered. "When we took the ship to the docking facility, after fixing everything and loading up our cargo, First Officer Lepsi 'n I were fortunate to spy a ship with black smudges painted on the aft panels. I went to examine closer 'n noticed the contours of the Fo'wo' symbol underneath."

Craze took cargo to mean the aviars had the chocolate bars stashed on board. "An actual Fo'wo' vessel?"

"Yup. It surprised us, too. We reported it to the Elstwhere patrollers 'n Assembled Authorities. Alarmed 'n having no available ship to go after the smugglers, they asked for our help. We had to agree. Can't have the enemy flitting around the Backworlds." Absolutely not. Craze's jaw tightened. "It's against the treaty 'n an insult."

"Most certainly. The Authorities was kind enough to offer us compensation for our patriotism," Lepsi said. "We assured them it wasn't necessary, we would defend against the enemy no matter what, but they insisted."

That was good news. Craze would recover some of his lost funds, depending on how much the patrollers valued this venture. "That was a fortunate event," he said. "Do we know where the Fo'wo's went?"

"Yup," Dactyl said, rubbing his left bicep as if spoiling for a fight. "The patrollers at the Elstwhere docks placed a tracker on the Fo'wo' vessel before it went through the Lepper, thanks to yous commanding officers' quick reporting."

That explained in more colorful detail how the aviars had gained some leverage, and why Craze wasn't currently in jail. "To where?"

"Way out on the Edge," Talos said. "The stop is called Mortua. A graveyard of ships."

Craze didn't like the sound of that.

✦ Chapter 18

Craze prepared to hibernate for the rest of the trip through the Lepper. He was exhausted from atmospheres he wasn't used to, clandestine affairs, an attack of claustrophobia, and scrubbing down the spacecraft. He'd just settled under the covers when he heard Lepsi and Talos in the living area. It only took a few steps to reach the door separating them.

Craze waved at the aviars to come over. "That patroller guy around?"

"He's keeping an eye on things up on the bridge," Talos said. "He's a Backworlds Assembled Authorities lawman with an impeccable record, always getting his fugitives. Kind of worries me. We'll end up in situations with a lot of bothers until we get rid of him."

Craze leaned on the doorframe, crossing his arms. "Not much we can do about it, except go along 'n survive. Hey, 'n thanks for gettin' me out of custody."

"You crew, mate," Talos said. "A ⌐Ⴑ⌐
it was an obligation."

Craze would accept that explanat
but knew he and the aviars had
alliance deeper than business. The ⎯⎯⎯⎯⎯ ⎯⎯⎯⎯ ⎯⎯⎯
done for him proved it. Unlike Bast, they deserved
his loyalty, and he vowed to show it moving
forward.

He kept his voice low. "So you got the
chocolates? I saw you escape."

Talos scratched at his sharp beak of a nose. "We
got the wrapped bars. We heard they mealworm
cakes."

"Did you check?" Craze chewed on the inside
of his cheek.

"We unwrapped one." Talos giggled, leaning in
closer, rubbing his thumb over the pin on his lapel.
"It was chocolate."

"Great shit!" Craze clapped his hands. "How
many did you get?"

Talos held up a cautionary hand. "Fifty-three
bars. We don't know whether they all chocolate
though."

With what the patrollers had shown Craze on
Elstwhere, the aviarman had a reason to be wary
about what they had taken away from Mr. Slade's
Emporium.

"We should unwrap the others," Craze said.
"Where'd you put them? I'll help." He took a step
into the living area, anxious to find out how badly
he'd been duped by the Jix and the smugglers.

"If we open them, they exposed to rotting,"
Talos said, his lips drawing to one side in a grimace.

:n they lose all their value."

Lepsi held up a finger, signaling he might have the solution. "If Mortua has a med bay, there's a surgical laser we can use to inspect under the casings 'n foils. It then reseals the holes."

Talos frowned, pressing his long body against the wall. "It's a shipyard 'n that's what it's known for. If it has more than a med kit, I'd be surprised."

"So we may not be able to find out on Mortua." Craze rubbed at his chin. "But someplace out here on the Edge will have what we need."

"Yup," Talos said, "until then we carry on." He pulled at the lapel sporting the badge with his beloved motto.

Patience had never been a strength of Craze's. He hated the idea of waiting and probably for a big disappointment. All of his investments had evaporated, as dried up as the mealworms. It kicked at him, bunching his muscles into knots.

Maybe the pay from the Assembled Authorities would make up for some of the loss. He had to ask, fingering the tab in his pocket, hoping the aviars intended to share. "How much did you get paid to chase after these Fo'wo' bastards?"

Talos took out his tab. "Forty-two thousand chips. I'll ping you your third now. I was waiting for Dactyl to give us some space."

Craze glanced at his balance to make sure it went through. Fourteen thousand chips was less than Bast had given him, but better than nothing. "I appreciate it guys… friends." That's what Craze wanted the aviars to be. He held out his hand for Lepsi and Talos to shake.

Lepsi shook with a big grin, clapping Craze on

the back as he did, laughing, a good-natured fellow despite those stupid songs. "Federoy will be envious when I report a pal like you. Plant your face in it, brother."

Craze chuckled, sticking his tongue out at Federoy's image when Lepsi held it out. "You got it better than he does. He'll find out soon."

Talos also shook hands. "The Edge is a dangerous place, mate," he said. "We can all use as many friends as we can get."

"Mate." Craze grinned. Then he explained how Verkinn could hibernate. "Wake me if anythin' comes up, otherwise I say goodnight until we arrive at Mortua."

He returned to his bunk, sinking under covers that cradled him as softly and warmly as Yerness's embraces once did. A pleasure he would never know again. At least not with her. Sighing, he told the computer to wake him three hours before they arrived at Mortua.

His overworked body began to shut down, his heart beat and lungs slowing, his blood flowing like ice five. His thoughts stopped, except for the hope that the chocolate they'd stolen would turn out to be chocolate. His last musing, "I'll get you, Bast."

✦ *Chapter 19*

The force of being spat out of the Lepper System plastered Craze to the back of his seat on the bridge. He had hibernated through the nine days it took to travel to Mortua, a small, rocky orb no bigger than an insignificant moon. It orbited a cheery, little star that shone too tiny and dim to be seen from the solar system next door. No water or plant life showed on the surface of Mortua, but Sequi's scans picked up a dome surrounding the docking facility.

Six other planets resided in the system, trifling and fractured, little more than boulders. The passage from the Lepper exit to Mortua was riddled with their remnants. Some of the refuse among the rock and ice was mechanical—ships and ship parts reeling in the unfiltered sunlight, cartwheeling and tumbling.

Talos sent a greeting to the docking facility asking for permission to land. He didn't get an immediate answer, so placed the Sequi in orbit around the craggy globe, going round and round with the debris of dead ships.

Hollowed out haulers afforded glimpses of destroyed interiors, bygone events with flame and explosions the crews could not have survived. Craze averted his gaze from the violence, finding no comfort in barracks and crew seats floating by themselves. Dead consoles twirled with seized-up engines and discarded hull plates. It didn't bode well for him and the aviars, or for whoever inhabited Mortua.

"Do you think the Fo'wo's harmed them? The folks on the planet?" Craze asked.

Dactyl tugged at the sleeves of his beige shirt. The cuffs had been shorn off to accommodate his short arms. "No… maybe. It's hard to remember they not like us." He plucked lint from his hard-used pants.

"How do you mean?"

"For the most part, from what I've heard 'n seen, they find it easier to cross the line 'n kill than we do. Although that's changed some since the war. Backworlders be more bloodthirsty than they used to be. Especially out here on the Edge. Most folks have guns that kill out here."

"Damn shame the Fo'wo's polluted us like that. Do you think it's true that the Fo'wo's always aimed to wipe us out?"

"I know so. My father said. He was a veteran." Dactyl absently rubbed his left arm.

The squat man claimed to be of the Quatten race. Bred for worlds with high gravity, he had to make a conscious effort to keep his strength in check. Craze found it amusing when the Quatten bent a chair, but he didn't dare laugh. A punch from Dactyl would hurt ten times worse.

"Thank him for his service." Craze meant it, appreciating every Backworlder that had taken on the fight. Maybe their side had officially lost, but they were still here.

Dactyl pressed his lips together until they disappeared. "He's dead now. Died a few years back. Complications from old war injuries. The Fo'wo's had no qualms about deploying biological weapons." His husky voice broke when speaking of his father, then heated up with anger as he mentioned the Fo'wo's and their dastardly armaments. He rubbed at his left bicep.

Craze winced. He'd seen the plagues and deformities on Siegna, which had its share of veterans. Every Backworld did. The Quatten seemed sincere, seemed like he was out here to make the Backworlds a better place by bringing the wanted to justice. Craze thought the profession noble, but only if the lawman moved out of his way.

Dactyl's dark brown eyes squinted at Mortua and the data Sequi's scanners displayed on the consoles. "To be polite, we give them some time to answer. Then we land anyway," he said to Talos. He pulled out a Backworld Assembled Authorities representative badge. "This allows us to land without bothers."

The four of them ate a meal together while waiting, dried fish flakes steeped in hot water and some hard bread. Craze gobbled down double portions, his body needy after the long hibernation.

Used to taking care of customers, he'd prepared the food, then cleaned up after. His willingness to serve kept up the charade that he was the lowest in rank on the Sequi. Well, that wasn't so much an act as he was in reality subordinate to the aviarmen.

"Not as low as the lawman thinks," Craze said to comfort himself. Right. He was a partner to Talos and Lepsi not a mere lackey.

Down in the common living space, he doused dishes with cleansing gel. He was wiping bowls and spoons dry when a reply from Mortua came in.

The signal was weak, making the message hard to decipher. Craze scrambled up the ladder to help, using his better hearing to make sense of the noise. He leaned over pressing his ear against the speaker. "He orders us to take Berth 10B."

"Anything else?" asked Talos.

Craze listened to the repeating missive several more times. "Nope."

Talos waved Craze to a seat. "Get alert, everybody. There's some real wackos out here on the Edge. There's no telling what'll be greeting us."

The aviars maneuvered the Sequi closer to the planet. The crags bloomed into mountain ranges and ravines, jagged and foreboding. Ice glistened off their facades in a dark frost that glittered only when starlight caught it. The Sequi drifted lower until the peaks threatened to spear its hull. Craze gripped onto his seat as the ship lurched without warning one way then the other in the air currents. The aviars wrestled against the winds, struggling for tenuous minutes to nestle the vessel into its assigned dock. The hiss of suction announced a secure seal.

The landing platforms and berths ringed the outside of the dome, which appeared too flimsy to protect the inhabitants from anything worse than a sneeze. The ship consoles read the air as cold and thin, factors that would make Craze's body want to hibernate. Despite his dislike of the cramped quarters, he had even less desire to walk around Mortua.

"Maybe one of us should stay behind 'n guard the ship," he said.

"First Officer Lepsi will do that once we greet the dock owner." Talos fingered the prized pin on his lapel. "We'll probably need your negotiation talents, Second."

Craze could see Talos wasn't of a mind to relent. Shit. Reluctantly, he followed the aviars down to the living level and through the corridor to the hatch. Dactyl stayed close on Craze's heels. The door opened to reveal a stark, gray world.

The fetor of recycled air without the introduction of anything fresh whooshed into Craze's wide nostrils. He took a step back, wheezing, trying to breathe only through his mouth. It didn't help. The air was too rank.

They walked through a short tunnel, then into the crux of civilization on Mortua. The clear dome arching overhead produced an eerie atmosphere, amplifying the bald sunlight, raw and severe. The thinness of the protection made Craze feel exposed and vulnerable, as if he'd be sucked off the surface to tumble with the clusters of orbiting garbage for all eternity.

The hangar inside the dome could easily accommodate five freighter-class ships. Most of the space, however, was taken up by row after row of scrap and parts, and two partial vessels. Craze tried to figure out whether the ships were being put back together or disassembled, but couldn't. Billboards winked around the perimeter, obnoxiously advertising a code every two seconds in every color and font.

A Backworlder clad in splatters of paint and nothing else greeted them. He was fleshy, of average height, and had six arms. "Welcome to Mortua. Currently, I'm refurbishing an intersystem hauler that's not designed to go through the Lepper. Have an old transport that is meant for Lepper travel to refit next if you want to wait around for it. Living costs are two hundred chips per person per day. That includes oxygen, but not water."

Steep price for rotten air. Craze thought the Backworlder should pay them to breathe the wretched stuff.

"We'll be keeping the ship we have," Talos said. He smiled tightly, standing straight and not showing any uncertainty, taking on the role of captain with aplomb. He plucked the prized pin off of his lapel and pocketed it.

Dactyl pushed Captain Talos aside, stepping in front of the aviarman. "We've come to buy something else. Information on yous last customer."

"I keep that confiden—"

Dactyl whipped out his badge, the one claiming he was a member of the Backworld Authorities, which was made up of representatives from almost every planet. It was the Assembled Authorities who had fought the war, then negotiated the truce with the Fo'wo's and enforced it. Now they kept the peace between the divergent Backworlds mostly by tracking down serious lawbreakers escaping planetary boundaries.

"They traded in their battle cruiser for a very nice mercenary vessel. I'm keeping the battle cruiser." The Mortuan gestured at an occupied docking slip opposite of the Sequi.

Across the hangar, Craze could make out the dark Fo'wo' spacecraft. Its shape reminded him of rocks jammed together. He couldn't figure out which were the aft panels, so couldn't find the painted over logo. Shifting his weight, he crossed his arms over his barrel of a chest, appearing intimidating until somebody needed him to do otherwise.

"We don't want the ship." Dactyl's fingers brushed over his left bicep. "We want to know where they went."

There was no sign of any other inhabitants other than the strange man in paint. The Backworlder's six arms sanded rings and gears, and what appeared to be parts to an engine. "They had me clear the Lepper to Wism."

Dactyl pointed at the code scrolling on every billboard in the docking facility. "That yous code?"

Four of the arms reassembled the sanded parts while the other two picked up more rusty pieces. "Yup."

"I'm pinging yous a thanks. Clear us for Wism, please." Dactyl punched icons on his tab then pocketed the device inside his long brown coat.

The Mortuan smiled friendlier. "In need of any

supplies? Spare parts?"

Talos reasserted himself, putting a hand on the lawman's shoulder and sending Dactyl to the background. "Yes. We could use an extra propellant cell—"

Dactyl yelled over the aviarman. "We need nothing. Clear the Lepper for us. Now."

Talos glowered at the Quatten, but Dactyl didn't care. He returned the foul expression. Inside the Sequi they argued over who had ultimate say on this mission. They bickered about it constantly most of the way to Wism.

Craze and Lepsi kept out of it, playing a lot of cards. That way they didn't appear to be listening as closely as they were. Anywhere else, Craze would have found the on-going squabble annoying. In the corridor of blue, it became entertainment.

✦ *Chapter 20*

Before they left the Lepper for their next destination, Talos and Dactyl came to an agreement. The Quatten would have authority over anything to do with apprehending the Fo'wo's, the aviarman would have ultimate say on anything to do with the Sequi and its crew.

"What kind of place is Wism?" Craze asked as they exited the portal of cobalt light. He hoped the planet would have a medical facility in order to find that laser they needed to assess the stash of chocolate-mealworm bars.

Talos stared out the view panel, following route beacons set out from the Lepper, punching in course corrections. Terms of the truce with Dactyl stated the captain would answer first. "Never been here before." His right eye and lips twitched rapidly.

Craze knew the tics were purely genetic manifestations and didn't rely on those to figure out Talos's real feelings on the matter. He checked the aviar's hands, which remained steady and out of his hair, the captain's true tell-all. If Talos wasn't hyped-up nervous, Craze saw no need to get wound up either. He leaned back in his chair, letting his legs stretch out long. "Nothin' to worry about, huh?"

His concentration on steering the ship, Talos was slow to answer. "It's just a place."

Dactyl clucked in disgust. "Yous can't wander about the Edge so ignorant 'n keep breathing. Wism is a horrible place loved by cut-throats, traitors, 'n dastards. There's plenty to worry about."

That wasn't at all reassuring. Craze gathered his legs back under him, sitting straighter. His hair stood up. He had to pet it for three whole minutes to get it to settle down. "Shit."

Dactyl crossed his short arms over his wide chest. "Unlike Mortua, it has a breathable atmosphere without a dome, but barely. We'll all be wheezing 'n needing frequent rest. It's a dark place, almost always in the shadow of its planet. That ringed orb over there."

The planet loomed lifeless and colorless with a ring that looked as if the globe had weakly expelled its last breath, a wimpy effort at generating interest. The moons around it didn't inspire anything greater than a sneer of contempt.

Craze didn't want to visit any of those worlds. "Wism is a moon?"

"Yup. Covered in black sand. Nothing but black sand that seeps into places yous don't want it," Dactyl said.

Craze shifted his weight tugging on the legs of

his coveralls. "You have some sort of plan? I mean we just not goin' to march in there like we did on Mortua. Right?"

"We gonna swagger this time." Dactyl seemed no taller standing, putting on his long brown coat, pulling at the lapels to settle the fabric around his wide body. He straightened his holsters.

Maybe the Quatten wasn't serious. For several minutes Craze waited to see if the lawman would crack. Dactyl's expression never wavered though. Not once. Dammitall, he meant what he said.

"We got nothin' to act haughty over," Craze said.

Dactyl rubbed absently at his left arm, something he did often enough that it made Craze wonder. Old injury? Something else?

"There's them bars yous took from Mr. Slade's Emporium on Elstwhere," Dactyl said. "Possession of chocolate gives any Backworlder the right to boast."

Shit. How'd he know about that? Dactyl might make them give the stash away or turn it into the Backworld Assembled Authorities. Craze sucked in his lips, organizing imaginary bottles on a dream shelf that seemed like it would never be realized. Rum with rum. Short to tall. Spiced to dark.

Talos ran a hand through his shock of blue, mouth pursing. He chanced a glance at Craze. Craze shrugged.

Dactyl chuckled. "I wasn't sure until now that yous took some. Yous all just ate a meal of guilt. It seeps out of yous every pore."

"The stuff concealing the frizzers was mealworms," Craze finally dared to say. "Isn't anythin' to swagger over."

"Not every bar was. When yous have docked 'n secured the ship, meet me down at the hatch." The lawman climbed down the ladder, leaving them to wonder.

Great news and misfortune all grotesquely entwined to hear that not every bar was a mealworm cake. Even just a few genuine chocolates represented a major fortune. The rub was whether they'd be allowed to keep any. But, hey, the patroller didn't know how many bars they'd taken. No reason they had to fess up to the whole lot, and way out here, Craze imagined Dactyl's disappearance could be easily arranged, especially if Wism was as rotten as he claimed.

Craze could tell the aviarmen thought the same thing. The three of them smirked at each other. Craze bit his lower lip to keep from cheering. He figured Dactyl hovered down there listening, but he couldn't help pumping his fist in the air a couple of times.

Lepsi whipped out his tab and sang in a bare whisper. "Eat that Federoy. You a stupid boy. Eat that Federoy. Face full of hemorrhoids."

Craze laughed at the inane rhyme, which encouraged Lepsi to get more outrageous. The aviarman stood, repeating the lines, swishing his hips, smashing the image of his brother against his backside.

Talos joined in the high jinks, beating the stale, smelly air inside their vessel with a raised fist, grinning. "Fortune keeps twisting our knickers. Huh?"

A shrill signal blasted over the Sequi's speakers,

stopping their revelry. It was a warning from Wism that coming any closer without contact would be considered a hostile act. Talos opened a communications channel to the docking facilitator.

Music blared over the speaker with the greeting. "Identify."

"Sequi, small passenger transport, coming from... Elstwhere." Talos raised his voice to be heard over the clamor on the other end. "Request docking."

"For what purpose?" The reply sounded gruff and rancorous, wary and suspicious.

Talos took his prized "Carry On" pin out of his pocket, and placed it prominently on the console where its comforts could be easily seen. It kept the quiver shaking his hair out of his words. "Trade 'n shelter." He almost barked it, matching crusty with crusty.

A dry cough cut through the din of bad singing and out-of-tune instruments. "Shelter from what?"

Talos didn't blink when blurting, "The Assembled Authorities. Bastards tailed us to Elstwhere. Heard we can lose them here."

Snort. "Must have something good to trade?" An iota of interest leaked into the last couple of syllables.

Talos let out a long, slow exhale. "Better than good. Bars wrapped in stamped gold foil."

"Shut it!" the dock facilitator yelled at the merrymakers on his end. An abrupt hush fell. His next sentences echoed clear as fresh-scrubbed air. "If you lying, we reserve the right to shoot you. Take Slot 12-24."

The threat was unmistakable. Craze gulped,

hoping the rest of the bars weren't mealworms. Wism wouldn't be forgiving.

Talos didn't break, sounding as confident as a sunburst. "Aye. Meet you at the bar."

When the connection cut, Craze asked. "How'd you know there's a tavern? Thought you've never been here."

"It's a constant out on the Edge." Talos steered the spacecraft toward the cluster of shadowy moons. Craze couldn't see a difference between one and another. "There's always a bar."

Good to know that when folks came out of the Lepper they expected a drink. Craze nodded. "Soon I'll have the best one the Edge has ever seen, a true destination."

"With folks coming from all over to trade their wares," Lepsi said, assisting Talos in guiding the vessel.

The aviars brought the Sequi in low, skirting over the ebony sands swirling into a dusty wake beneath their passage. Craze watched as particles glistened when caught in the ship's lights, dancing and winking like flirtatious gals. The landscape stretched in soft undulations of fine grit, gentle wave after gentle wave of black without variation until the Sequi began the approach to the docking facility. There the sands ended abruptly in an oasis of bedrock, dipping into a steep canyon. Along the ravine walls glowed spots of orange and yellow, the lights of an austere city. A rickety bridge linked the two sides, but Craze didn't see any movement. It was as if they headed to a ghost town. The Sequi braked and turned for a ledge protruding from the rock face.

"They live in caves?" Craze said. "Doesn't history say the Fo'wo's once lived in caves? Before they became civilized? Hrrmph. Depends on one's definition of the word I guess."

"Ain't that the truth," Talos answered. "Barbaric horde of inferior genes is all they is."

"True as the Lepper's blue." Lepsi nudged the ship closer to the walls, openings gaping like hungry mouths and flaming eyes. "Looks like a huge skull about to swallow us."

A very unhelpful observation, Craze thought.

Lepsi rubbed at a tic under his eye. "You did a great job getting us a landing, Talos. However, I'm worried we won't live up to their expectations. What if the first bar they open is mealworms?"

"We give them the opened one we know is chocolate," Craze said. He remembered the rough crowd in the bar on Elstwhere, friends of the Jix who probably called Wism home. "Put on your darkest clothes before goin' to the hatch. Black if you've got it."

Craze went down to his bunk, switching out his cheery red suspenders for forest green ones, and his white shirt for a caramel-colored one. It was the darkest shirt he had. Lastly, he put on the gray duster, wishing he'd selected a black one instead.

At the hatch, the aviars smeared cleansing gel mixed with dirt into their hair and onto their shirts. It darkened them, but they were a far cry from black. Dactyl had on a black hat with all his brown. The effect was lacking, but Craze couldn't fault them for it. It was the best any of them could do

The lawman handed them each a holster complete with a revolver. "Strap 'em on," Dactyl said. "This is one of them Backworlds where bullets rule. These folks won't hesitate to use theirs. Try to avoid such a situation. 'N whatever yous do, don't smile or get too surly. Surly enough will do." He rubbed at that left bicep again, facing the hatch with a steely mien, as if he could wrestle the rocks and win.

Craze wasn't sure what surly enough meant, but he figured not behaving the coward was part of it. He thrust his chin up and hooked his thumbs on the holster strapped to his hips, mimicking the Quatten. The hatch slid open. Despite the show of bravado, his knees knocked threatening to give out.

✦ Chapter 21

Dactyl took the lead leaving the Sequi. The aviarmen flanked his sides, and Craze brought up the rear.

One scrawny kid stood there with a scowl on his face that could crack a hull. "This way, assholes." He strode off through a tunnel in the rock lit by safe lanterns sunk into the floor.

Maintaining the same formation, Craze and his companions followed. The air was cool, threatening to be damp, but not quite making it. It smelled sour and sharp. The sharpness probably came from the ventilation system. Craze could hear the fans rumbling below the din in the near distance. Folks roared and barked, slapping things and laughing. The laughter was cold and unsettling, the tones mocking, seeking to cause pain and humiliation.

Craze hitched up the holster, his fingertips grazing over the revolver's handle. Then he stopped, wheezing, heart hammering. He braced himself against the nearest rock wall, laboring to catch his breath. His hand rasped over jagged chiseled edges biting into his palm, raising welts.

The aviars and lawman huffed too, but hadn't run into the difficulty Craze had. His coveralls pumped against his chest in a maniacal rhythm. The thin air might as well have been absent as far as his body was concerned. It wanted to shut down and hibernate. He yawned.

"No time for sleeping." Dactyl held Craze up, pushing him toward the gold light and flickering shadows seeping around the bend. "You can rest in the bar with a beer in yous hand. Not much farther to go."

Craze's legs buckled. He swayed, chest constricting, inhales useless. He'd not make it, not without sitting still for awhile. The kid leading them, glowered at him, sizing him up, determining him weak. The smile his young, reedy face offered came off as smug and stupid. Craze met the glare, narrowing his eyes. He gripped the revolver handle and spat. The kid ran.

"What did I tell yous on the ship?" Dactyl stomped a foot. "Now he's gonna tell our contact we Flatsies to be pushed around. That doesn't help us none at all."

Leaning against the wall, Craze panted, doing his best to rally. He winced when Dactyl mentioned Flatsies—tab-thin Backworlders feeble as newborns. "You go on then, you 'n the aviarmen. I'll go back to the ship."

Talos shook his head, whipping out his prized pin. Orange words with wings on blue. "Carry on. We need your skills. C'mon, Lepsi, help me out."

On either side of him, the aviars shored Craze up and walked him toward the light and the noise.

Lepsi hummed, a few words escaping here and there. "Lean on yo mates... heavy brother... carrying on... wha wha la."

The corridor opened a little wider into a hellhole. Broken tables and chairs splintered into spears as drunk folks sparred with one another. Ale sloshed out of the tankards in their hands, and everyone wore black as Craze had predicted. A good number of the crowd even had black teeth.

Craze estimated about fifty Backworlders were crammed into a tavern sized to comfortably serve thirty. He hoped this wasn't considered a large establishment out here on the Edge. He'd never get his revenge on Bast if that were so. Shit.

Talos and Lepsi set him on a stool at the counter. His breathing came a little easier and his pounding heart slowed. He calmed himself further by concentrating on the bottles of booze on the shelf behind the bar. Organized completely wrong, he reordered them in his mind. Blue with blue. Short to tall.

Dactyl requested ales from the bartender and paid for them. The four of them turned, their backs solidly against the bar, surveying the other patrons, sipping the brew.

Craze had been wrong earlier. The sharp smell came from the shit in his cup and not the ventilation machinery. It tasted like mildewed ship hull. Worse. He wrinkled his nose and discreetly spat the beer back into his mug.

A wall of a man sauntered over to them. He wasn't tall, but burly and muscular, like he did nothing but lift chunks of rock. His head was shaven and painted with disturbing images of blood, knives, and shattered bones. The art spread down onto his cheeks, a permanent mask. He wore a sleeveless shirt and black pants ripped at the knees. His feet were bare and black, painted like the aviarmen's hair. His fingers sported rings with spikes and razors, making the threat of his punches more painful.

"I want to see what you came to trade. Now." The tone of his voice matched the rock the room was carved from.

Maybe he had eaten through it to create the city on Wism, Craze mused. "What you got to trade for it?" He couldn't help taking the lead on negotiating. The art of the deal ran strong in his blood. The coveralls were finally able to manage his equilibrium, and he stood.

"Down. Don't yous listen." Dactyl shoved Craze back in order to stand nose-to-chest with the dude big as a boulder. "We'll tell yous our terms when we decide 'em." His glare didn't waver from Rock Man's. A timeless stare down. The Quatten pushed up the sleeves of his coat, his hand lingering longer on the left bicep, the shoulder lurching, before he settled himself with a determined, grim expression.

Rock Man shifted his weight first, a hint at respect, putting a little space between himself and Dactyl.

The lawman bared his teeth, inching forward. "Here's a sample." He handed the big man the bar of chocolate the aviars had unwrapped. "We'll be back with our terms in two hours. In the meantime, we want to walk around Wism without bothers from anyone."

Rock Man sniffed the chocolate bar and arched his brows, satisfied the goods were as promised. "Consider it done, little man."

Dactyl didn't even hint at a flinch. The condescending name didn't bother him. He thrust his chin at the far corridor. "Keep that as a token of our intentions to make a good deal. Clear us a path. Now."

Rock Man's fist closed over the chocolate and he hollered above the noise in the bar. "These special guests of mine. Keep your mitts off 'n make sure everybody else knows it."

Space opened up around Craze and his friends. When they stepped toward the intended tunnel opposite from where they had come in, the gap between them and the Wism derelicts stayed constant, like they were encased in a bubble.

Dactyl led the way to other docking berths, searching for the Fo'wo' vessel and the Fo'wo's. Craze couldn't keep up. His body couldn't match his will. The lawman and the aviars left him wheezing on a crate in a storage bay.

They walked away, Lepsi singing one of his made up songs. "Don't asphyxiate for me, Verkinn guppy. We need our fortunes… 'n not by dying."

Craze would have rolled his eyes if he could see straight. Hand over his chest, he fought the urge to hibernate, gasping to get more air and remain conscious. A clang made him whirl about. The sudden action made things worse, bringing on a wave of dizziness. He fell to the ground, mouth working, sucking in need of what it couldn't find, as if he had been thrust into a cosmic void.

✦ *Chapter 22*

Craze found himself staring into the face of a gal with chrome-hued skin. Tears and blood streamed down her cheeks. Her lips opened wide as a Lepper portal. She screamed and screamed and screamed. Craze had to close his ear holes, choking, trying to speak. He couldn't get enough air. He could only lay there blinking at her, hoping his expression conveyed he meant her no harm.

"Please," he huffed. "Please... I... no... hurt... you."

She stopped shrieking to listen to his choppy plea, sniffling. "You look familiar. Have we met? I think we met before. Not here though. I hate this place. I haven't been here long, but I know I hate it."

Her pink irises raked down Craze, making him feel naked. There was a glow behind them not entirely natural. He noticed cybernetic plugs at her elbows. The mechanical halves of her arms were missing though. The same was true of her knees and legs. She had no hands or feet, helpless on the floor like he was.

He recovered enough to speak better. "We haven't met. I'd remember you. I don't like this place either. You OK? You look hurt."

"I suppose I'll live if my next master lets me. I don't know why I still need a master. I can think for myself now, decide things for myself. This obedience thing sucks. They make me do things I don't want to do." She sniffed, crinkling the bruises on her otherwise lovely chrome cheeks.

Her partial arm hit against his coveralls. "That's how I know you. I made those. Don't you remember? My master kept me on Siegna several weeks so I could make those for you. They not working well enough here, huh? That's not because I did bad work. Wism is just hard for anybody to breathe on let alone someone like you. There's a canteen in the corner with the rest o' my stuff, a tea I brewed. It should help you. Drink it."

Wow, she could talk. He'd never met a cybernetic Backworlder before and couldn't judge whether this was normal. "It wasn't me you met on Siegna," he said, "but I've been told my pa 'n I resemble each other a lot." He looked around, trying to figure out which corner she meant.

"Your pa? What a small arm of the galaxy. What's the chances of us running into each other like this?"

"Freaky." Craze pushed himself up to sitting, slumping against the nearest crate. The effort made his head swim. He noticed her arms and legs thrown into the farthest corner across the bay. Of course, way over there. He crawled toward them. "Who did this to you?"

"My master is unhappy with me. Says he's going to sell me." Her weeping filled the storage room, until she wailed like an alarm. "I don't want to stay here."

Craze pushed the cybernetic arms and legs at the gal. They slid easily across the floor, bumping up against her floundering form. He followed after them, rolling and slithering. He figured out how to plug in an arm for her. After that, she was able to put on the other arm and her legs herself.

She leaned over and kissed his cheek. "Thank you. Now drink the tea." She held the canteen to his lips.

He panted on the floor, hand pressed over his aching chest, taking a tentative sip. Her concoction tasted like over-ripe socks in piss. He pushed the flask away. "That tastes terrible."

She sobbed. "Oh. I mean nothing bad. Honest I don't." Her shoulders shook with her sorrow. "You won't buy me now, will you? I had hopes. You seem like a good man."

Craze ripped a cuff off of his shirt, wiping her face of blood and tears. "Don't be so sad. I know you mean good." He took back the canteen, swallowing down half of the contents, swiping away stray dribbles with the back of his hand. "See."

Her words heaved out in sputters. "I work so hard to please, but my masters is always angry 'n mean. I don't know how to be better. Why do I have to have a master?"

Craze didn't know, didn't understand her kind.

He could empathize with not feeling good enough for others, and he was pissed someone would stoop to beating her and leaving her like this.

He put an arm around her shoulders, pressing his side against hers, offering comfort. "You deserve better than this, Sweetheart. I'll help you. OK? Does that make you feel better?"

Her dripping pink eyes raised up to meet his gaze, her lower lip trembling. "You will?"

Shit, he was such a sap. That was exactly how Yerness had manipulated him, acting all needy and sad, proclaiming him hero. What would this gal do to him in the end? Leave him here naked and dead, all his chips in her pockets? Well, OK, she didn't have pockets or clothes or much of anything and she didn't have that I'm-going-to-devour-you spark in her eye. Besides her tea worked. Already his lungs ached less. This gal wasn't out to use anybody for anything but to end her misery. Craze could relate.

"Yes 'n I can feel your tea rallyin' me." He drank more from the canteen.

"It's great I can aid you in payment for helping me. I have to confess, I was afraid you was an awful criminal when I first saw you 'n again when I saw the coveralls. Your pa said they was for a no-good lowlife he didn't need hanging around. A man who caused trouble 'n would do his family harm. You don't seem like that."

Damned Bast. Bastard-ass waste of gene manipulation. "Let's not talk about him. He's a dastard as bad as these folks here."

"He did you wrong, huh? I'm sorry I had a hand in all that," she said between sniffs.

Craze handed her the piece of his shirt. "You didn't know. I'm Craze, by the way."

She wiped her face, then held out her see-through mechanical hand. The circuits glowed pink when her fingers moved. "I'm Rainly."

They shook. Despite the unnatural origins of the limb, her palm felt soft and warm, like anybody else's. Craze could detect a pulse thrumming through her wrist. She was more than a compilation of cybernetic parts.

"Nice to meet you.," he said.

She picked at the edges of a crate, peeling off splinters of compressed fibers. "How you going to help me?"

✦ *Chapter 23*

Craze struggled to hurry, wanting to remain unseen. The threat of hibernation kept slowing him down, and they kept smacking into dead ends.

"Looks like we have to cut through the bar," Rainly said.

Chances were slim they'd get through the tavern unnoticed and unscathed, no matter how drunk the patrons were. Most thugs had a sixth sense when it came to someone trying to pull something over on them. So Bast had taught him, and he had seen it for himself on Siegna, where the crowd resembled credentialed nannies compared to the gang here on Wism.

Craze leaned against the rough-hewn wall, huffing. "We didn't try that way yet." He pulled himself along, his hands gripping on the rock, dragging him to the left.

Rainly put an arm around him, assisting. "That leads to the boss man's place. The big dude with the colorful face."

"Oh." Craze stopped. Shit.

"You said they was mighty busy being drunks in the bar. Maybe no one will notice. Like you said." She winced when she tried to smile in an encouraging way, the beating she took earlier swelling her cheeks.

She would have to remember the stupidest thing he said and bring it up. Dammitall. Craze thought over their situation some more, coming up with nothing new or brilliant. Maybe with his coat on, she'd pass through as just another drunk. Probably not. The skin, hair, and eyes gave her away. He stuck out just as much in tan clothing head to ankle. Tan was better than chrome and white though.

He took off his shirt, arranging it over her hair as if a scarf. The cold of Wism pricked at his skin, shooting like pikes into his joints. "Act like you belong. Do what they do. Don't cower."

"You clever." She giggled, patting at the makeshift hood.

They stumbled back toward the bar, resting just outside. Craze peeked around the corner. Four bodies slumped over the entryway, too drunk to stand. A clump of folks in the center gyrated like insane snakes, singing at the top of their lungs. "Die. Die. Die. Let's die tomorrow."

Cheery lyrics. Blending in with that crowd would be his and Rainly's best shot at getting through the tavern with minimal notice. He swished his hips side to side, loosening up, tightening his grip on her hand, pushing himself off of the wall.

"What you doing?" whispered next to his ear.

Craze jumped, reeling about on his heels, heart hammering, pulse racing, breath escaping him in a gasp. "Talos!"

Rainly squealed, high and shrill, like when Craze first bumped into her. She didn't stop. Craze squeezed her hand, petting her cheeks, telling her she had to shut up.

Too late. The dancing folks quit singing and dancing, pivoting as one toward Rainly's screams, licking their lips, smelling prey. Shit.

A man as formidable as Rock Man moved Craze's way, fists clenched, his lower jaw tightening until rigid. "That's my property. What you doing with her?"

Rainly whimpered, trembling like the sands outside in a breeze. Craze pushed her behind him. "Found her discarded in a trash heap."

"She wasn't tossed out. She was stored, dumbass."

Craze spoke out the side of his mouth. "We could use some help here, Talos. Find Lepsi 'n Dactyl. Hurry."

He could see he and Rock Brother were evenly matched in size. If he had proper lung capacity, he'd not worry about squaring off with the guy, but he didn't. Apologizing was out. He'd try that surly-enough thing the lawman had preached, hoping he'd hit it right. "Didn't see no sign sayin' so. She's mine now." He dodged to duck around the guy.

Rock Brother's meaty hand stopped Craze. A punch followed, connecting square on Craze's jaw, sending him reeling backwards, exposing Rainly.

She was yanked back to her master's side. He

cracked her one across those already badly beaten cheeks. "What shit you pulling on me, Toots? You forget to tell him who you belong to?"

She shook, her lip quaking, blubbering an insensible, "Me, me, me, me me."

He twisted her wrist until she stopped her sniveling to scream. Loud as a siren her distress had to be heard all over Wism.

The folks in the bar laughed, closing in, wanting a piece of the blood about to spill. Craze scrambled to get onto his feet, huffing and panting, closing his fists.

Egged on by the crowd, Rock Brother punched Rainly three times, knocking her onto her ass, stomping on her until she quit resisting and fell silent. "Tell me you sorry. Tell me!" he kept saying.

Craze charged at him, using all his lung capacity to haul him off of her, clawing, pulling, hitting. Rock Brother whirled, pummeling Craze with fists and boots. Craze did his best to ward off the blows, but the fight quickly winded him. His body threatening to stop, he fell to his knees. Whomp, whomp, whomp. Pain crashed into his temples, his jaw, his nose and lips splintered, agony exploded in his ribs, then in a knee. In a last desperate attempt, he pulled his revolver. Eighty pointed back at him, hammers clicking.

Shit.

Rock Brother grabbed Craze by the hair, which hurt more than the punches. The living hair's abuse made Craze wail like a girl, a vulnerability as glaring as the need for enriched oxygen. He yowled, in more torment than any steel-toed boot could deliver, blinded to any other need. Rock Brother took the advantage offered, wrenching the gun out of Craze's hand, pressing the barrel against Craze's temple. Shit fifty times over.

"Hold on there," Dactyl strode into the fray. "We can make a deal."

The original Rock Man joined his brother, placing a boot on Rainly's head. "Chocolate won't save you from your asshole friend stealing 'n causing trouble. Just ain't a good idea to go around taking from others on a world like this."

"We ain't friends. Just doing business together. Nothing more. It's his first time out here on the Edge 'n he's woefully uneducated as to our ways. Certainly, we can find a way to forgiveness." Dactyl held his hands up, inching closer. The aviars flanked him, copying the lawman's every move.

"Stupid to team up with Flatsy-assed babies." Rock Man nodded and his brother clutched more severely at Craze's sensitive hair, taking another swing at Craze's brutalized nose. The sting welled in Craze's eyes, fueling cackles and guffaws from the crowd.

"A chip per punch." Rock Man held up his tab for the pings. "Five to take out some aggression on robot girl."

Dactyl ground his jaw, spitting. "I got the better deal 'n yous know it. Chips don't come close to what I got to offer."

"Mercy comes with a heavy price," Rock Man said, calling one lady forward to kick at Craze and allowing one of the drunken men to paw at Rainly.

Craze tasted blood in his throat, gasping for a full breath, his fingers clawing against the floor to get to Rainly. He'd get that man off of her. Damn his body for failing him. He put all his effort into moving closer, reaching for her foot. A boot shattered his hand, but Craze barely noticed, his determination on the chrome gal. Her cries were so quiet and she didn't twitch. It worried him. His hand useless, he employed his elbows to inch across the floor. The asshole's boots assaulted him as he did. Whomp. Whomp. Whomp.

"Ten bars of chocolate," Dactyl said, "for merely letting him return to our ship. He'll bother yous no more this visit."

Rock Man nodded another man forward to punch Craze. "He'll bother us never again."

Craze didn't feel the slug to his gut. All the spots of anguish cancelled each other out in a numbing agony. Only Rock Brother's grasp on his hair made any impact. Craze groaned, his mangled hands desperately trying to pry his tormenter's fingers loose.

The lawman's gaze flickered to the sniffling Rainly and the two women using her as a smack sack. "Thirty for the both of 'em. That'll bring yous more chips than this moon is worth."

Rock Man called the next man forward, pulling the two women off Rainly. "She's not so easily bought. I can make a lot of money off of her. We get lots of lonely visitors here on Wism."

Craze's sight narrowed to one tiny slit. He watched the next punch from the ceiling, as if he were no longer inside himself. Everyone's words hummed, and became indistinguishable, a language beyond his understanding. The next blow caused black to edge his vision. He'd welcome losing consciousness. He longed for it.

Dactyl's jaw twitched.

"We offer forty," Talos said. "No one in this section of the Edge has that many chips. The kind of wealth that's hard to come by out here."

The aviarman was bold. Craze appreciated it, but he groaned. That was almost all of their stash— the means to their trade routes and taverns, and Dactyl's desire to catch the Fo'wo's and make them pay. There'd not be enough left for the lawman to buy a lead.

Rock Man laughed. "I ain't much into mercy today 'n seems my customers like the entertainment." He called the next two customers forward. One for Craze. One for Rainly.

Dactyl tugged his coat off, throwing it on the ground, ripping off the left sleeve of his shirt. Images in ink stained his left bicep. He thrust the shoulder toward the leader of Wism, making sure the man saw the tattoo and understood what it meant. "You'll stop this now, or suffer the consequences. Yous saw my arm 'n really get what I mean. Yes?"

Rock Man's voice quivered. "Yup. I see."

"You'll take our deal for these two 'n you'll take another ten to forget we exist."

On the lawman's arm was a depiction of death. Dark portrayals of suffering people—writhing, sliced open, impaled, their guts spilling, and a river of blood. Skulls decorated the banks and a symbol involving entwined snakes repeated around the whole scene. It had meaning to the thugs here on Wism. It had none to Craze other than he might live through this.

Rock Man stopped the next bar patron from

walloping Craze, and sent the rest of the crowd backwards with a snarl. "I accept. Send Quasser my regards."

Fifty bars of chocolate. That left only three. Maybe enough to buy a permanent docking berth on some forsaken world, someplace where all their dreams would wither. Shit.

✦ *Chapter 24*

Back on the Sequi, no one spoke a word. They slipped back into the Lepper, cleared for Pote. It was a planet the aviars had been to before that had a good medical facility and few bothers.

All the injuries had Craze slipping in and out of hibernation along the way. The memories of being carried to and from the ship and to the hospital were pure fuzz. He could recall ceiling passing by overhead and a gal sniffling. Rainly.

"Rainly?"

"You need to rest," a lady all in orange said, placing an oxygen mask over his face.

The influx of air made his lungs ache less. When he felt strong enough to sit up, Talos stared at him from a chair across the room, rolling that prized pin between his fingers. His expression was crestfallen, but not devoid of all hope.

"Where we at?" Craze asked.

"Pote. You 'n Rainly needed tending for your

injuries. Yours was really bad. Cost us the remaining three bars, mate."

Shit. That explained Talos's glum face, but not the glimmer of optimism. "I'm sorry, dammitall, more sorry than I can say." Craze ran a hand over his sore hair. It hurt too much to do anything but lay flat. Since he had avoided cutting it to escape unnecessary pain, the strands without the usual waves and curls tumbled down to his hips.

"No panicking. We'll find another fortune," Talos said. He seemed to mean it, too. He quit fidgeting with the button, pinning it on his coat. "Carry on. That's what we'll do. Don't argue with Mom. She knew her stuff. She used to tell me sometimes things come along more important than trade routes 'n riches. Here we be at one of those sometimes things."

Were they? What had become more important? The creak in his side when Craze moved brought a few of them to mind: he'd lived, he'd get a tomorrow to seek his vengeance on Bast, and he'd rescued a sad gal. Maybe even given her a chance at some happiness. Dammitall, Talos was right. And it mattered a lot that the aviarman was here, standing by Craze, watching over him. It was a connection stronger than Craze ever had with his Verkinn family. A partnership worth as much as the sheeny chips they had let go.

"You think?" Craze asked.

"Life. Freedom. Good friends. A working ship 'n the best of folks to sail it with. We'll be all right. There's places we can go 'n start over." He held out Craze's tab with one hand, pinging it from the tab in his other. "We still have the money the

Elstwhere patrollers gave us, which means something on some worlds. I made a list."

Taking the proffered tab, Craze glanced at Talos's data. Six planets offered homesteads and businesses at prices within their means. Six. A galaxy of possibility had narrowed down to those few options.

"We need another propellant cell for the Sequi though." Talos fingered the pin on his lapel. "So you can scratch the first place off."

Five options. "Can we get more chips if we keep chasing after the Fo'wo's?"

Talos shook his head. "Dactyl got fired."

"How come?"

"Because I made the choice to give up any chance at getting a reliable lead on the Fo'wo's to help yous sorry asses 'n I lost the shits. Then there's the issue of bartering with stolen goods," the lawman said, leaning into the room, nodding at Talos. "We about ready to go? Rainly's anxious to start the home search. She's never had one before. Ain't that a shame?"

"You seem OK with how things turned out," Craze said to the Quatten.

"It's only a job 'n money." Dactyl's long brown coat was gone, but he had sewn the sleeve back on his shirt, covering up the symbols that had scared the piss out of Rock Man.

Who exactly was Dactyl? Craze swallowed wrong, choking on his own spit. He held up a hand as he fought to get enough control back to speak. "Only? 'N who's Quasser? What's that tattoo you got mean?"

"We all have a past. I won't ask about yous

dastardly pa unless yous want to say. Yous don't ask about before I was a lawman unless I want to say."

"OK. What will you say?"

"I joined up with the law to make up for things I'd done. Saving yous 'n Rainly was the right thing to do no matter the consequences. Yous make up for things…"

Craze could tell he'd learn nothing more. Not at this point. Maybe some day in the future when they'd all had many more adventures together. "Well, thank you. I appreciate it 'n I'm pretty sure Rainly does, too. Where is she by the way? She OK?"

"She's fine, thrilled to hear yous well enough to leave today." Dactyl saluted Talos, fist to chest. "The Sequi's ready to go, Captain. Except for the fuel cell."

"I'm about to go buy it." Talos stood with a sigh.

Craze knew he owed the aviarman for helping with the failed heist, for getting him out of custody, for giving him a place when he had none, and for not running off when things got rough. Nice things. Craze would keep his vow to return the kindnesses to Talos and Lepsi. "I have some really nice bottles of booze in my pack," he said. "One or two should get what we need. Save your chips. Put option six back on the list."

"Really?" Talos's face brightened. "Running into you on that transport from Siegna turned out to be great fortune, mate. Life isn't dull with you around. 'N to think I didn't want to be anywhere near you at first." Laughing, he buzzed Lepsi on his tab, telling him to get Craze's pack and meet them at the trader's bay.

With Dactyl's assistance, Talos helped Craze to the shop. Craze aided in negotiating the hooch for the propellant cell. His friends then guided him back to the Sequi, strapping him into his usual seat.

Rainly beamed at him. She wore a halter and shorts made from Dactyl's coat with a patch over her heart that was Craze's cuff. Over that bit of material she wore the lawman's old badge, literally advertising her heart to the world. "You starting to look better. I'm so glad." Her bruises were black as a cosmic void, but no darkness could tarnish her radiant disposition.

It made Craze smile, despite wishing most of his body parts would find new homes and leave him in peace. He squeezed her hand. "Good to see you, too."

Sitting up so long made him moan, which led to thoughts of misery and the lost chocolates. They had left so much wealth behind on Wism. Maybe. Or maybe they didn't. If they didn't, that was a problem. One as big as the Rock Man and his brother. "What if most of those bars was mealworms? Those dudes will come for us. Won't they?"

"As long as Quasser lives, we've nothing to worry about," Dactyl said, settling into the chair beside Rainly's.

"You ever goin' to tell us who he is?" Craze would risk a slug or two to sate his intense curiosity.

"Yous may hear whispers of Quasser from time to time, but not from decent folks. He's somebody yous don't want to know. Not even by somebody else telling yous about him. Drop it, or we gonna talk for the next few hours about yous pa 'n Yerness."

Craze pressed his lips together, biting back his myriad questions. He didn't want to pollute today or tomorrow with Bast and Yerness. Dactyl was right. The past was the past. "New beginnin' right here. For all of us. Where we goin', Captain?"

"Carry on!" Talos slapped the console. "We've been cleared for Danysovia. First stop on the list of possibilities."

Craze peered at the planets Talos had pinged onto his tab. Little to no information besides the names and locations graced the InfoCy data files. After Danysovia was Lleteboor, Foradil, then a place called Pardeep Station. Exsix and Awjiscar were the last ports of opportunity.

Worries coated Craze's palms in a cold, slick sheen. If Mortua and Wism lay outside their monetary means, what kind of holes in the galactic arm would these planets be? Shit. He wiped his hands off on his coveralls.

"Ready?" Talos clicked the course into the ship systems, taking the Sequi up toward the Lepper.

The streams of cobalt blue reached for the vessel to whisk them away from all the tragedies and failures, inspiring the resurgence of hope in Craze. Not every stop could end in disaster and disappointment. Could it? Nah.

And maybe there was nothing wrong with those six places besides their being so far out on the Edge. Just remote and unsettled, the new frontier, nothing worse than that. As the Backworlds healed from the war, they'd expand once again, and the Edge wouldn't remain the boondocks forever. No. Untapped potential waited out there, and Craze would grab it along with his new-found brothers and sister.

"Danysovia here we come," Lepsi sang out, waving Federoy's image at the view out the spacecraft. "Give us chips. Give us chips."

Dactyl held Rainly's hand. They shared a smile, intimate and warm. Seemed they'd found something as precious as chocolate on Wism.

It made Craze miss Yerness for a split second. Then he realized it was the intimacy he longed for and not her. Someday he'd find the right gal. He knew that and knew he'd be OK. The aches for lost love, Siegna, and home eased. He'd lucked into a cozy new life with a new family. One that actually looked out for him and shared this same journey. On a quest for better and for healing, together they would find it. One of those worlds on Talos's list would become home.

Craze felt a tinge of excitement, wondering which one. "Let's go."

If you enjoyed reading The Backworlds think about leaving a review.

Want to be informed of upcoming releases and receive discounts on ebooks? Sign up for M. Pax's newsletter at http://mpaxauthor.com

Comments from readers always welcome, mpaxauthor@gmail.com

A sneak peek at:

Stopover at the Backworlds' Edge

Book Two

✦ *Chapter 1*

Incoming! The message vibrated through the floor, a low coo penetrating deep into Craze's subhearing. The drone of an engine grew louder until the floor shook, reducing him to a speck in the galaxy's workings. A reminder that liked to crop up twice daily when he wasn't hibernating.

He rolled onto his back. Orange lights joined the alert, blinking at a frenetic rate. They fringed the mishmash tavern and quit flickering when his foot kicked up at the switch on the wall. Through the plexiglass skylight he saw the telltale flash, a cough of cobalt disturbing the anemic blue sky. The brightness stung until moisture built up in his eyes and he sneezed. Ship!

He inhaled deep, canvassing the scents in the ventilation system, seeking something different. Something revealing today would be the day the portal finally brought fortune, the means of revenge, the goal he'd clung to since his pa kicked him off the Verkinn homeworld three years ago. Had it really been that long?

i

"Damned Bast." He spat. "Someday I'll know wealth big enough to make you choke."

Craze's shoulders shrugged, shaking off the dregs of a nine-day hibernation, and he cursed not being woken sooner. "Fo'wo's be damned." Nine days of not pouring a single drink wasn't anybody's definition of success and certainly not his. At this rate, Bast would die before Craze made the man woefully sorry. He groaned, wondering how destiny had landed him here... for the three thousandth time.

Pardeep Station had been fourth on Captain Talos's list of possible homes. Hole of dust as it was, it hadn't been as bad as Danysovia, Lleteboor, and Foradil. Six months of hopping around dung heaps and worse, searching, Craze had agreed with his shipmates —Talos, Lepsi, Rainly, and Dactyl — that they'd find no better. Especially once a Foradillan showed him images of the two worlds left on the list of possibilities. Indisputable proof there was much worse out there.

Yup, this dust ball was the best Craze and his friends could afford, once they got past the crusty, old caretaker — a war veteran still fighting the enemy in imaginary battles. When the old coot finally became convinced they weren't Fo'wo spies, Craze negotiated homesteading fees for the lot of them.

Purchased with what they'd been paid by the Backworld Assembled Authorities to chase after some smugglers, Craze acquired space for his tavern, a permanent docking berth for their ship, the Sequi, a trading post for Talos, the position of dock facilitator and assistant for Rainly and Dactyl, and mining permits and a land transport for Lepsi to take up prospecting. Lepsi had hoped to find some pocket of value on Pardeep Station, something to set up an export business for himself and Talos. It never came about.

Craze built his bar at the base of the docking facility from scraps and unwanted materials, his friends helping him to get it together and make it presentable. In exchange, he assisted in setting up their new homes, although Craze couldn't bring himself to call Pardeep and his tavern that. It settled more like a stepping stone in his heart. Someplace until something better came along. He'd been here two and a half years, and the moon hadn't grown on him at all. In fact, he despised it more by the day.

To make it all worse, Lepsi disappeared a year ago. Never came back from one of his explorations. No trace of him had been found anywhere, not even his transport, coloring each day since with a sorrowful ache.

Mouth dryer than a dust pit, Craze ran his tongue around his gums, then stretched. He slipped on his boots and pushed himself off the mat laid out in the plexiglass foyer in front of his tavern door to prevent anyone from sneaking in without his knowing.

Tugging his suspenders up and his sleeves down, he readied for customers and the influx of chips, bright sheeny chips, which could transport him off this backworld's Backworld to a better port with greater opportunity. Someplace with trees and potential, someplace that wasn't the last stop for one hundred fifteen light years.

Rolling up the thickly woven filaments he used as a bed, he tucked it under the salvaged bar spliced together from discarded walls, doors, and the bodies of land vehicles topped by a counter poured from a resin he'd formed and sanded until it gleamed without blemish. Despite the discordance of the materials, a rich and mellow style had distilled and the tavern sparkled clean with everything in its place.

Behind the bar, he poked between the tapped kegs of mead and malt to find the means to contact the other residents of Pardeep Station, to make sure they'd seen the ship coming through the Lepper. Not many Backworlders – those bioengineered to take advantage of the scraggly planets the galaxy offered as less than ideal habitats – scrimped by here. Pardeep Station was rough and not fully formed, uninspiring and lacking in imagination, impersonating a stain.

Craze hit the summons to his neighbors, an icon on his tab – a thin flexible data device the size of a card. "Lepper opened. Ship headin' in," he yelled out to those who earned a living off travelers as much as he did.

His courtesy to his friends done, he shut off the connection and sauntered past five tables of different shapes coated in thick beige polymer. Returning to the plexiglass door in the vestibule, he waited on the approaching ship, wondering what kind of business to anticipate. What class of vessel would come out of the portal ripped into space by the Lepper System? How many people would be on board? A massive transport filled with the very rich kind of folks was what he dreamed of, knowing full well that was unlikely, as those kind rarely came to a place like Pardeep Station.

He shouldered into the door's heavily scratched surface, which jerked open with a scraping noise after a shove and a kick. The air bit on the inside of Craze's outspread nostrils, the sharp twang making him rub at the side of his nose.

The roar of approaching engines jostled the loose, gravelly soil, the granules jumping and skittering, sending up a dust storm of supergene proportion. His black eyes squinted through the commotion, making out a more densely packed column of dirt mingling with the ship's wake, adding to the coming tempest.

The intensifying frenzy of dust sent a tremor of trepidation through him. Logic told him the darkening cloud was one of his fellow Pardeepans coming in to make a few sheeny chips off the tourists, yet his emotions ran rampant, sensing portent, perhaps for no other reason than it was more interesting to think so than not.

Craze filled the doorframe he leaned against with muscle and height. The splayed placement of his cheeks, eyes, flat nose, and prominent mouth allowed him to live comfortably on hot worlds rife with organics choking the air. His ability to hibernate let him survive in places with extreme seasons, seasonal being the key. The yearly changes on Pardeep went from cold to bitter. Craze made do though, like the other hardy souls who worked on this orbiting lump of arid rock.

His charcoal waves neatly rebraided themselves into a single plait, then lay still. The living hair gave him some popularity with females and saved him time grooming. Beyond that he'd never figured out what purpose that particular modification to his genes served. Catching insects maybe?

Pardeep's dust-laden air tasted of chalk and tin, coating his tongue and thick lips. The incoming vessel swooped lower, gliding toward the docks rising twenty stories above his tavern. The bronze hued edifice glinted in the sunlight, otherwise the facility blended in with the soil. It was the only noticeable blip of civilization on Pardeep, and Craze would hardly call it that. Maybe if the incoming spacecraft brought more settlers he might.

The ship, as large as an interstellar-class freighter, cast a great shadow which darkened the landscape and his view of the world. Shaped like a dumbbell and colored in rust patches, the hull of the spacecraft clung to a brittle and aged patina, showing little promise of fulfilling his ambitions for prosperity, but there at the tail blazoned a crisp logo. Freshly repainted, a circle half blue and half green dominated the aft panels, rekindling a little hope for something more than the arrival of destitute derelicts. A vessel like that could hold up to a half thousand folks.

Craze's pulse quickened. That was a lot of chips. Chips he desperately wanted to add to his coffers. "C'mon!" He pumped his fist at the sky, then forced himself to settle down. The incoming ship could easily hold a half thousand cobwebs and crumbs instead.

As the spacecraft approached, the squall of dust sped closer, rising ever higher, somersaulting and churning, turning darker and blacker, reaching up to devour the docks, the bar, and Craze whole. He backed inside the plexiglass vestibule and slammed the door, unable to peel his sight away from the storm roaring at him like a wall.

He gulped, cursing the Pardeepan twit creating the monsoon. "Nobody'll be able to take more than three steps from the docks, dumbass."

When his words consciously sank in, Craze's lips parted with a smack. "Oh!" He didn't want people wandering about, perhaps tempted into taking one of Pauder's idiotic tours. Nope, he wanted them in his bar and staying put.

The entryway had the only windows in the tavern. As the swarm of dust raced toward him, he was glad of it. He braced himself for the onslaught and ground his teeth. Pebbles scoured the exterior of his place and sliced fresh scratches into the door. Then came a series of explosions, close and thunderous.

Boom. Boom. Boom.

Shit.

Craze closed his ears and ducked.

✦ *Chapter 2*

On his knees, Craze retreated farther into his tavern, heading past the jumble of beige-coated tables and chairs toward cover behind the counter. "Damn you, you Backworld reject."

Now he knew who added to the uproar out there. The old fool Pauder, who believed the war hadn't ended. Craze needed to get Pauder to stop before the tourists veered away, opting for the next stop along the Lepper System.

He chanced leaving his cover, inching his way back over to the door, cracking it open to shout through the slit. "If you scare off business, old man, I'll come huntin' you."

Another volley of gunfire boomed, followed by twangs of ordnance bouncing off the hull of the docking ship. Craze glanced up, because only a well-armored spacecraft could ward off what Pauder threw at it, and they were rare.

Craze could make out the faint illumination of a

protective shield and heavy-duty rivets securing armored plates. Weapons bays ran down the ship's belly. Not a freighter or transport, it was made for war. He'd never seen a battleship before, and rubbed at the back of his neck. The trickle of uneasiness from earlier intensified.

"Get them. Get the Fo'wo's." Pauder's tones rattled with fury, punctuated by four more shots.

Craze rolled his eyes. "The war's over! You damned coot." He sure hoped so, hoped those weapons bays didn't become something to worry about.

In a skull-hugging helmet of thick fabric, goggles, and a gas mask, Pauder jumped down from his all-terrainer jacked up high on treads which churned up more dust than the incoming ship. The old man's dark skin shone, the moisture produced by a hide comprised of bony shields and rings. His sharp fingers, engineered for hunting, gripped the trigger and leveled the bazooka at Craze. "I see yar piss-ass ship, vermit. Die like a Fo'wo 'n scream for me." He cackled in an unforgiving manner, then lowered the barrel as big as Craze's head. "Oh, it's ya."

Craze crossed his arms over his keg-shaped chest. "Yup, me, not a natu-bred Fo'wo. Not that it matters. The war's been over sixty years now."

Those old injuries didn't do Pauder any favors, he'd been blown apart and put back together too many times to have all his sanity. Another problem, his kind lived too long. What passed three generations ago for most, played like yesterday in his recollection. And he'd struggle through another century or more before letting Pardeep put the tired issue to rest.

A taloned finger shook under Craze's nose. "'N the good guys lost, son. Look at this hellhole."

Craze couldn't argue.

"That decoration on the hull ain't no decoration, Mr. Barkeep. It's trouble. Plague-inciting, warmongering trouble. The symbol's covert ops of the Foreworlds. Fo'wo's is here, come ta erase ya from existence. I'll be waiting back there." Pauder pointed at a storage closet against the back wall smack in the center of the shelves of booze. "When they come in 'n is about ta let yar brain matter loose onta the floor, I'll jump out right then ta spring ya from their clutches. Bam. Bam. Baaam!"

"You ain't shootin' a bazooka in my bar," Craze said. "I don't care if the ship is Fo'wo's. But it isn't. Maybe a new passenger line from somebody who got a great deal on that ship, or some hotshot mercenaries. Maybe even Fo'wo pirate scum, but not an enemy army. No way."

Medals hung around Pauder's neck — three bronze and two silver — casting light on the underside of his prominent chin. He thrust the bronze award he most prized at Craze, shouting his years of heroism without words. "Yar so damned ignorant, it hurts my teeth. Oh, the enemy is wily, Craze. Wilier than ya can ever imagine. There's no truce. Not in their minds. Not until we all dead." He crammed himself into the storage closet and slammed the door. Muffled words flitted past Craze's flat, indistinct ears. "We should have some sort of signal."

"Like, come out of the closet?"

The door flew open, rattling the bottles shelved on either side in a precise pattern of size, shape, and color. Blue with blue. Short to tall. The coot jumped out waving the bazooka at the tavern's corners, teetering off balance until he compensated for the head injury he refused to acknowledge, claiming it had never happened. Perhaps the root of his problems. "Where they at, son? Where they at?"

Craze rubbed his meaty palms over his face, his eyes itching from the kicked-up dust. "Get back in the damned closet, you rejected pile of gene splicin'."

Just in time. The tavern shook and a siren blared. Pardeep's docks joined with the incoming ship, snagging it fast to a berth above, announced by loud grates jarring Craze's hair, then his lips. He stood with his legs wide, and knees loose. The crocks and bottles rattled, but nothing fell or cracked.

When the quaking ended, Craze took his place behind the counter and powered on all the lights. "Time for business."

Lit up as if for a celebration, the horseshoe of a bar glowed. The top glittered, reflecting the shine. The bottles lined up on the mirrored shelves gleamed, glistening with promises of exotic tastes and altered moods. Above the bar a rack hung, holding rows of crocks and bowls, canisters of ingredients, and blue bulbs reclaimed from scrapped ships. The bulbs dangled from the edges, a cascade of ambient radiance, casting blue dots on the counter. A sign topped the rack, protruding up toward the ceiling in a bold proclamation.

Illuminated in yellow and orange, it read, "Craze's Tavern."

To draw in the folks disembarking, Craze unlatched an enclosure under the bar and fished around inside for a handful of ricklits. The plump insects screamed, "Rrrrickl't, rrrickl't." Bright yellow with iridescent blue spots, the bugs thrashed their squat bodies around in his wide palms, antennae kicking in the air. Craze threw all but one into a roaster.

The roaster sat in a cubby surrounded by an elaborate air flow system. Craze switched on the cooker and the fans. Within thirty seconds the delicious odor of baking ricklits kicked out all other smells in his place. Irresistible. His mouth watered. When his stomach bucked in a loud plea, he popped the one ricklit he'd left out between his lips, biting down on the tasty head, eating it raw, enjoying the crunch and burst of cream. Flavored much like perfectly deep-fried chicken, a customer had once said.

Chewing on the bit of protein, Craze tied on his apron. His rugged hands, which had put many wayward patrons out the door, washed the covers and sip spouts. Soon after, the jar parts got a rudimentary rinse in the basin of disinfecting gel. The yellow wasn't the right shade of yellow, long past its prime, dingy and faded, glopping like gravel because of all the grit stuck in it. Gently, he set each cleaned crock on a rack on the bar top, lining them up for the incoming customers.

The door scraped open. In walked one person. She stretched like the first rays of a moonrise, not looking anything like a Fo'wo or a covert agent. On her heels followed an entourage of breezy shadows, which closed in on her, dimming her and her silver light.

Craze rubbed at his eyes, wondering what had gone wrong with his vision. Did her shadow just move? Where was everybody else? He had enough tables to seat three hundred, stools at the counter to accommodate another two dozen, and could cram in more for those willing to stand, especially if Pauder didn't hang around to police things.

"That big, old ship just for you?" he asked.

The shadows cleared, finding walls and corners to cling to. Silver shimmered over the visitor's hair and skin, flowing like her kaleidoscope dress. The tinkling pitter-patter of falling glass beads followed her onto the bar stool in front of Craze. She perched delicately on the round cushion upholstered in a weary red. Donning a forlorn smile, she spread her empty hands. "Drink for a thirsty traveler? It's been a long journey from Bofeld. You know it?"

"No. Got any of them pretty, legal tender like chips?" He searched her top to toe, looking for something of value. Her empty hands and oily hair didn't appear very promising. Craze sighed, hoping her ship would take off soon, not wanting to deal with her begging for hours on end.

He feigned being very busy, washing crocks and placing them back on the rack he'd just taken them from, wiping off kegs under the bar and bottles shelved on the back wall, stirring the cooking ricklits. He shook some spice into his palm and added it to the roaster, dusting off the sticking granules of red powder on his hand onto the apron. His stomach rumbled as the fragrant aroma filled his nostrils, and he thought it a pity ricklits didn't reproduce faster.

Out the corner of his eye, he caught a dark shape flickering. It swooped over the counter, pooled around his feet and leapt, reaching for his face. Craze jumped, dropping the stirrer in his hand.

His customer cackled.

What crap was this? Shit. He'd be more pissed if she'd caused him to drop a bottle. "Tricks'll get you nowhere, dearheart. Currency here's chips."

"I'm tapped out, I'm afraid. But have I got a story for you. It's worth ten drinks, but I'll tell it to you for one."

If Craze had a water ration for every time he'd heard that, Pardeep Station would feel like a first-class world. "It won't be nothin' I haven't heard before."

"You haven't heard dis," she said.

✦ *Chapter 3*

Craze examined her more carefully. Slits in her neck expanded then disappeared. Gills. A Water-breather? Supposed to be extinct, shit, they were the worst kind of Backworlder, if the rumors were true. They'd turn on anything if the advantage shifted right, cracking through their own children's chests to steal their hearts if that would keep them alive longer. So the stories went. And what were those creepy shadowy things with her? A chill crept over Craze's shoulders, souring his stomach, especially at the way she preened as if she had a right to take up space at his bar. Not if she didn't have chips.

Her movements swayed like kelp in a tide and her eyes glinted a polluted yellow like the gel he'd washed the crocks in, shining with a sickly quality as if she was in dire need of some sun. He should throw her out on her scrawny ass. Only he didn't want the likes of a Water-breather gunning for him.

What if the rumors weren't exaggerated?

"Just one drink... what's your name?" She gawked at the lighted sign over the bar, her lips twitching in amusement. "Is dat your name? Craze? What kind of name's dat?" She laughed and snorted, slapping the counter until she remembered why she sat there. Begging. "C'mon, Craze, show some compassion."

Her pleading didn't change his mind. In no mood for games and definitely not having the patience to hear any stories, Craze had to figure out how to play this right. If he lent her an ear and a drink, he might come out no worse. Yet he feared a trap, sensing he had already stepped into it just by letting her into his bar, and no matter what he did, he'd sink farther into it.

While he thought the potentially dangerous situation over, his hard-used hands bunched and loosened, washing and wiping. Pipe-like fingers smeared the excess gel off on the well-used apron which was a deep red, a color that hid a lot of history. His rigid suspenders holding up the tan coveralls sported the same shade of crimson. The garment kept his blood warmed and properly aerated with organics, a must for him to manage in Pardeep's thin air.

He tugged on the suspenders, mulling over whether she posed the threat rumored about her kind, concluding that above all else he was a businessman and he wanted off this hellhole, to go somewhere he didn't need to wear special coveralls. He couldn't start making exceptions about payment. Every supposed extinct Water-breather would be here on the next transport. Not the kind of business he wanted to conduct. Certainly not a path to success and prosperity. Wouldn't get him any closer to the revenge he wanted either. "Nothin' of worth to trade, no drink, dearheart."

She bristled at the tone, then licked her lips, her fingers shaking and a stench radiating off of her of stale hooch, brine, and blood. Her puckering frown slowly changed into a simper, dry and sticking, proving her great need for the drink. Proven again as her lips spread wider into a grin, setting aside Craze's unwelcome answer in less time than it took her to slide her fingers along the bar as if it were somebody who meant something.

Her lithe fingers left the smooth composite counter, walking onto her chest, stroking along her deep neckline, then lowering the zipper on her simple multi-color shift. The pigments swirled hypnotically. "Give me the drink. If you don't like the story…"

Her offer hung between them, the dress pooling at her waist, exposing cool silver skin. Standing up, she let the kaleidoscope outfit drift to the floor, her long legs stepping out of it, her cheeks free of the flames of embarrassment. She retook her place on the barstool. Perched like a Siren upon a water-sodden boulder, something regal sparked in her eye, but only for a moment.

The solicitation didn't surprise Craze. If the Water-breather hated him, she'd still present herself as tender. He could tell, it sat on her like the decades' old fetor of recycled air in the docking facility. Didn't keep him from checking her out though. Yup, she was definitely a Water-breather. Her damp iridescent skin, revealed from chest to toe, did little for him.

He crossed his hulking arms over his broad chest and unfurled a few curls to purposely fall over one eye to hide his distaste. His brown thumb gestured at the door. "I don't deal in that type of currency, dearheart."

He enjoyed watching the certainty of her proposition fall from her face. Anger flared in the set of her mouth until her longing for a drink forgave all faster than the last transport had taken off for the central-most Backworlds. The hint of temper relaxed into a flirtatious pout. "Name your price." She bent to pick up the dress.

Craze flashed a tight smile, his thick lips parting into a toothy expression. "What else you got to offer?"

The garment balled up in her fist, she leaned over with her breasts propped up pert on the counter. "What the crew of dat ship's looking for 'n how to keep dat vessel full of thugs from killing you." She placed a tab on the counter showing the same ship that had just come out of the Lepper with a white circle and red stripes on the aft panels where the freshly painted green and blue sphere now was. "They Fo'wo's, barkeep."

Some of Craze's hairs pulled free to stand up. He petted them over a minute to get them to settle down. He had a run-in with Fo'wo mercenaries once before that hadn't turned out well, the smugglers he and the aviarmen had chased out to the Edge. They couldn't still be drifting around out here, could they? The Backworlds Assembled Authorities had to have caught them by now. "They not allowed here. The truce."

The Water-breather cackled. "The truce means nothing to 'em. Haven't you heard?"

Craze had heard and was surprised Pauder didn't leap out of the closet to gloat over being right. "You full of it, dearheart."

"You just hoping. 'N here's something you don't know, someone here's been feeding information to the Fo'wo's. I read the reports on all of you, young Verkinn from Siegna whose father booted you out 'n married your gal. You live to get your vengeance on him. You'd trade your soul for it. 'N you'll get the chance today."

She shifted her weight, dragging her bossoms along the bar top, smearing its perfect gloss. "Your Verkinn kin want to sprawl over the Backworlds once more. They branded you a leecher at your father's bidding, the worst thing a Verkinn can be, to force you into going after their dreams. You not doing so great at it. Been nine days since you last opened dis tavern 'n poured a drink, barkeep. Yup, I know. It's true. A real live snitcher right under your nose."

Snitcher ranked the highest among all the crimes. The lowest thing a Backworlder could do was betray other Backworlders to the Fo'wo's. The only crime considered as bad was using a horrific Fo'wo' weapon called a frizzer. None of Craze's friends struck him as capable of such dastardly deeds. They all hated the enemy, most vowing to shoot them on sight.

He wiped the smudges she'd left off the counter. "Snitcher?" He waved an arm in her face.

A simple search could have turned up the moon of Elstwhere's he'd grown up on and his family connections. But how'd she know when he last poured a drink and all the details of his shameful history before Pardeep? The idea that someone on this heap reported back to the Foreworlds disturbed him. Not many lived here and he considered them all good friends, family even.

This had to be some sort of trick like the shadows. No way did anybody here work for the Fo'wo's. Besides, there was nothing to tell. "On freakin' Pardeep? What the hell for? Take a good gander at this place, dearheart, there's nothin' to find."

The tavern and docking facility suffered from dust and a lack of notice, waiting for its shot at a heyday, echoing Pardeep's loneliness through the bays and hallways. Craze couldn't imagine anything of worth anywhere on the moon. If any value existed, someone would have discovered it by now.

"Something's here of prime importance. Leftover ordnance from the war. Ply me with drink while I tell my story, then I'll tell you what you want to know. 'N you can keep the tab." She nodded at the data and communications device she'd set down on the bar. "It's a nice one."

Craze took down a bin from the rack over his head. It was filled with thin rectangles. "Keep your stinkin' tab. I got nicer models 'n the last thing I need is another one."

"Fine." She picked up the slim bit of technology. "My information is still valuable. The Fo'wo's have something here worth a lot of chips. More chips than dis tavern is worth."

Fortune always interested him, but with reservations from her. "Why in all the Backworlds should I trust the likes of you?"

A shadow bobbed in his peripheral vision. Craze wheeled about to face it, but it appeared the lights and the Water-breather's words messed with him. Nothing out of the ordinary moved. Still, he didn't like her, wanted her gone.

"You don't have very many options here, barkeep of Pardeep. They going to march off dat ride, make you find what they want, then leave you all in a lake of your own blood. Then they'll move the Lepper 'n Pardeep will disappear."

"Bull—"

Cold slapped across his back like a reprimand. The gust burst in through the door, rattling the stale air and tired shadows. A scraggly little thing came in with the wind, the next puff threatening to whisk her off through the Lepper to Elstwhere.

An enormous coat hid half of Meelo's face and covered her down past her toes. Craze knew it to be Meelo by her size and the bulky, one-of-a-kind outerwear which gave a whole different meaning to deep pockets.

All bundled up, Craze knew she'd prefer to never face the world. When she had first arrived on Pardeep Station, it had taken almost six months to get her to say a word and meet his gaze, and back then she worked and lived in his tavern.

Her mangled little hands kept to themselves, tucked inside her sleeves, and her lower face stayed concealed always by the high collar. He figured her mouth and chin might be mangled, too, but it didn't stop him from feeling soft about her.

He waved her forward. "Bring anythin' for me?"

The girl shuffled from foot to foot when she

could move no closer to Craze, the bar being in the way. Calloused hands pulled several vegetables out of her coat. "R-rootbaggers up. Now weather's changed." It was almost a monologue from Meelo.

Craze checked over the dirt-encrusted short hair sticking out in all directions and the watery blue eyes to determine whether she did OK or not. She appeared weather-beaten, but no more beaten than that. Ever since he'd agreed to give her work, he'd felt responsible for her. He remembered the doctor who had brought her, a lady he had great respect for and tried to woo. It hadn't worked out with the doctor lady the way Craze had wanted, but now Meelo occupied those same thoughts. So the loss to him wasn't acute.

"I'll roast one up now 'n save the rest for a stew," he said. At some point, when Meelo needed something, Craze would talk Talos into getting it for her. That was their deal. For now, he set a serving of the freshly roasted ricklits down on the counter. "Did you want hours today?"

"I-if you need me."

"I'm always glad for help, especially from you. For now there's just the one customer though." He jerked his head toward the Water-breather.

"I can see 'n hear you," Dearheart said.

Craze winked at Meelo, ignoring the Water-breather. "My charm has no bounds."

Meelo climbed up on a stool and pulled the bowl in against her chest. She crunched down one, then a handful, making yum noises. Somehow she did so without the coat peeling away from her mouth in the slightest.

Craze set all but one rootbagger in a cache in

the floor, then retrieved a large knife from under the bar. Hacking up the vegetable for the roaster, he bounced a wayward curl for Meelo's notice. She would often giggle when he let his hair move around in outlandish styles. He liked when she laughed. She didn't even snicker.

He paused and glanced up. With grave concentration, she gobbled down ricklits, too hungry to notice his curls. He frowned, clearing his throat until he caught her notice. "Dearheart here claims she has a story worthy of a crock of somethin'. My brew or the rotgut?"

The Water-breather licked her lips, staring at the taps. "It's worth ten crocks of your finest mead 'n then some."

"Tell you what, if your story is good enough, Meelo gets the say-so, I'll give you a crock of my good stuff when you through." Craze hoped that would get the Water-breather's designs off his back. Whatever they were, he wanted no part of them. "You agree, Meelo?" He wished he could see her lips. He'd been fantasizing about them the past fifteen months.

Meelo's weak blue gaze scurried over the Water-breather. "C-Craze brews a nice mead. Must be some story."

"It is," the Water-breather said sitting up straighter, her sallow eyes piercing into Craze's. "I was a settler on Bofeld. There's only five of us left. I never want to see the other four again. I'd probably kill 'em. I hate what I am."

ABOUT M. PAX

M. Pax is author of the sci-fi series, *The Backworlds*, and the new adult urban fantasy *Hetty Locklear* series. A Browncoat and SG fan, she's also slightly obsessed with Jane Austen. In the summers she docents as a star guide at Pine Mountain Observatory where the other astronomers believe she now has the most extensive collection of moon photos in existence. No fear, there will be more next summer. She lives in stunning Central Oregon with the Husband Unit and two lovely, spoiled cats. Want to connect? Visit www.mpaxauthor.com

28143795R00100

Made in the USA
Lexington, KY
08 December 2013